Italian Murder Mystery

A Rocky and Bernadette Murder Mystery

J.M. HUDSON

Contents

Tuesday, Day One

Chapter 1

Bernadette Mallow strode through the arrivals gate at Milan's Malpensa Airport and scanned the crowd. She spotted her partner, photographer Rocky Falconi, lounging against a pillar, hands in the pockets of his Italian cut jacket, long dark hair pulled back in a short, neat tail at the back.

She knew he'd be waiting, but actually seeing him added an extra spark of excitement to the week ahead. Her nerves were already humming about her second assignment with *Let's Travel* magazine, the thrill of spending a week in Cremona, the charming, historic violin capital of the world an hour south of Milan, and the buzz she'd picked up from her fellow passengers on the flight from Vancouver to Milan.

Of course, her excitement had nothing to do with the man in dark glasses whom she was walking toward. Absolutely nothing at all. She was just looking forward to a week of sublime music, amazing medieval architecture, and delicious Italian food.

Everything will be fine, she told herself silently for the hundredth time. This time she was prepared. This time there wouldn't be any trouble – not that the problems on the last trip had been her fault, but still, this time, no police. She straightened her shoulders. And absolutely no dead bodies.

As she closed the distance between them, Rocky pushed his shades to the top of his head, his deep brown eyes drifted over her and a slow smile slid across his face.

"Ciao, Mallow," he said, putting his hands on her shoulders and pulling her in for an air-kiss on each cheek.

At his touch, a current raced through her. More than just physical attraction – although that was certainly there too – she recognized a signal from her second sight. Hopefully not the, *something's in the wind* warning, but more, *something exciting is bound to happen*.

She returned his air-kisses and laughed. "Ciao. You're looking very–" she felt her cheeks flush. "Italian."

He looked like he belonged here, and apparently he did. Her editor Jen had told her that although Rocky had grown up in San Francisco, he had family just outside Cremona. This was one of the reasons Jen had chosen this location for their second assignment together.

Rocky draped an arm casually across her shoulders and spun Bernadette toward the baggage recovery belt. "Let's grab your bags and get out of here. I'm double parked."

"You have a car?" she asked as she wrestled her case off the carousel.

"A ride," he clarified.

Bernadette pulled up the drag bar on her bag and turned toward the exit. "A ride? With whom?"

"My cousin Niccolo drove me up. I got to Cremona a few days ago and I've been staying with him. I have a room in the hotel with you now, though."

They stepped out of the terminal and Bernadette paused for a moment and closed her eyes, enjoying the sultry breeze on her cheeks. The air felt more like summer than the cool October weather she had left behind in Vancouver. She took a deep breath. *Ah, Italy!*

But the moment was short. When she opened her eyes, Rocky was already walking toward a sporty looking black car that was indeed double-parked at the curb. Beside it, a tall man with long dark hair swept back from a high forehead was engaged in an animated argument with a security guard. Their arms were flying and their shoulders hunched toward each other.

The car was a two door. Rocky held the front seat forward and forced Bernadette's suitcase into the backseat. Then he gestured with a wave of his hand. "Climb in, partner."

Bernadette peered into the miniscule space and winced. "You've got to be kidding. That's not a back seat."

He grinned. "Welcome to Italy. It's an Alfa GTV. Nineteen ninety-six." He ran an appreciative hand along the admittedly sleek contour of the roofline above the door.

Accepting defeat with a shake of her head, Bernadette squeezed in beside her luggage.

As Rocky jumped into the front seat, the other man smiled, gave the guard a genial slap on the back, folded himself into the driver's seat and turned the key. The engine started with a throaty growl.

"You took long enough!" he said to Rocky in heavily accented English.

Bernadette clutched her seat as the compact car zipped into the anarchy of airport traffic, picking up speed surprisingly quickly considering it was so heavily laden. Once the driver had merged neatly onto the highway, he swiveled in his seat and held out a hand to Bernadette. "Ciao. I am Niccolo Falconi. Cousin of Rocky. I have heard about you."

"Ciao." Bernadette loosened one hand from her death grip on the edge of the seat to shake his outstretched hand, relieved when he turned his attention back to the road.

"We'll be in Cremona in an hour and a half. Maybe less," he said.

Rocky grinned back at Bernadette. "One-hour tops, the way he drives."

Niccolo hitched one shoulder. "It's rush hour."

He was right. The traffic was dense on the freeway that circled Milan. After a few minutes Rocky and Niccolo switched from English to Italian and Bernadette settled back in her seat letting the rhythmic, liquid sound of the language wash over her.

Her first job with Rocky, that week in Mexico six months ago, had been the most exciting week of her life. It was something outside her normal, struggling, single-mother existence, with a job with the magazine she hoped to make permanent and a partner who was, well, different from the men she knew back home.

Her eyelids drifted shut. She would have plenty of time to catch up with Rocky in the week to come.

Chapter 2

B ernadette awoke, sat up straight and rubbed the cramp in her neck. Dusk had fallen and, looking out the car window, she saw the dark, blank side of a tractor trailer, hovering far too close and going much too fast. Their cramped little Alfa zipped past it, then Niccolo hit the brakes and swerved in front of the monster truck to allow a sleek German sportscar to flash by.

"Where are we?" Bernadette asked, jetlag clinging to her brain like overcooked linguini.

Rocky turned in his seat. "We are almost there."

In the distance, the medieval towers of a town were softly outlined against the darkening sky and growing larger by the second. A highway sign flashed by overhead, blazing in the darkness: *Cremona 2KM.* They followed the exit arrow off to the right, took an overpass over the highway and headed into town.

At first the sidewalks were deserted, ground-floor storefronts closed for the night behind black iron gates. With every turn the streets grew narrower and the buildings grew older until soon they were racing through alleys with mere inches to spare on either side of the small car. In the darkness, golden lights overhead threw graphic shadows across the archaic façades of ancient buildings. Bernadette felt like she was flying back through time.

Leaning forward between the two men, she peered out the front window. Ahead, she glimpsed a church, glowing in the narrow space at the end of the road. A cathedral, from the size of it. The car sped toward the light until with less than half a block to go, they jerked to a stop.

"This is it," Rocky said. The men climbed out and flipped both front seats forward for Bernadette and her luggage to squeeze out.

She soon realized there is no graceful way to climb out of the backseat of a tiny European car, especially in such a narrow street, so she took Rocky's offered hand and concentrated on not twisting an ankle on the rough cobblestone pavement as she clambered out.

On the driver's side, Niccolo was cursing her suitcase which was wedged in the backseat. It finally gave way and the momentum flung him back against the stone wall of a building.

"*Prossimo tempo, i piccoli valigi*! Next time, bring small bags," Niccolo said, translating for himself, then continuing with an incomprehensible string of Italian.

Catching Bernadette's inquiring eyebrows, Rocky laughed. "I won't translate the rest," he said as he pulled his own overnight duffle and various canvas equipment bags out of the tiny trunk.

Niccolo grabbed Bernadette by the shoulders and kissed her soundly on both cheeks, saying, "Ciao and goodbye." He gave Rocky a back-slapping hug and was gone, the roar of the engine echoing off the dark, stone walls.

Feeling slightly stunned, Bernadette watched the Alfa speed away. "I didn't thank him."

"No need," Rocky said. He was already carrying his bags up to the hotel entrance, so she grabbed her case and followed, thumping it up the short, stone staircase.

Like the other buildings on the narrow street, the hotel presented an inscrutable façade: old stone, dimly lit windows, and a flickering sign above the entrance – *ALBERGO CREMONA.*

Inside, a clerk in a dark suit flashed them a welcoming smile from behind a black marble reception desk. Bernadette was relieved to let Rocky's smooth flow of Italian speed them through the check-in. Then the desk clerk turned and welcomed her in courteous English. Motioning toward the bank of elevators, he handed the room keys to Rocky, then added a few last words in Italian.

Bernadette wrestled her bag into the elevator and as the doors closed, leaned back against the mirrored walls. "What did the clerk say? Something about your cameras? *Due* cameras?"

Rocky laughed. "*Camera* is Italian for room. He indicated our rooms are very close together," Rocky said, raising his eyebrows suggestively over an otherwise deadpan expression.

She rolled her eyes, but before she could think of a pithy response, the elevator doors slid open and they stepped out into a darkened hall. Rocky hit a switch on the wall and the corridor lit up. At her door, he handed her a large iron key attached to a numbered wooden tag, then continued on to the next room.

Bernadette inserted her key into the lock just as the timed corridor lights went out.

Rocky stepped into his room and switched on the light, but before closing the door, he stuck his head back out into the hall and asked, "Hungry?" Right on cue, Bernadette's stomach growled. He must have heard it, because he grinned and said, "Meet you downstairs in thirty."

She nodded. That sounded perfect. She opened her door and fumbled for the light switch inside the room, but when the room sprang to life, she felt a twinge of disappointment. It was surprisingly modern. Generic, even. Could have been anywhere. She'd been expecting, hoping for, something older. With more character. Something *Italian.*

Dumping her bags on the bed, she pulled out her toiletry kit and stepped into the bathroom. Now this was more like it. Over-the-top marble with all the upscale modern fixtures Italians do to perfection. Thirty minutes would be about right; enough time for a quick shower but not enough time to get lured into bed.

Not with Rocky waiting downstairs with a glass of Italian wine with her name on it.

Chapter 3

R ocky took a seat at the hotel bar and looked around the room. It was very old-world, all gilt and mirrors and dark wood. He ordered a drink and settled in to wait for Bernadette. Thinking back to their meeting at the airport, his lips curled in a smile. She looked good. Her hair was longer now, brown curls falling below her shoulders. Tall and slim, the woman had class. He had seen her at her best, but also at her worst, and he knew she wasn't as cool as she looked.

He knew her secret. She had *the sight*. A second sight inherited from her grandmother that often seemed to manifest in a vague sort of premonition. Too bad she never knew what it meant. Rocky wore a talisman his Calabrian grandmother had given him when he'd started to travel, to protect him from that kind of sorcery. If he hadn't been a believer before, after the things that had happened on that first trip with Bernadette, he'd be a believer now. His eyes narrowed. He'd give anything to know what went on behind her fluttering lids when her eyes glazed over.

But in that one tumultuous week they'd spent in Mexico last spring, she'd found the cracks in his veneer, too. Cracks he hadn't realized existed.

They had gotten off to a bumpy start on their first assignment together but eventually, as the body count rose, their awkwardness almost disappeared. Things changed for him on that trip, and he had been thinking about her ever since.

This assignment would be different: a week in Italy, his second home, covering Mondo Musica, the annual, international violin trade show, and the Cremona Crown, a competition of arguably the best young violinists in the world. All set against the magical, medieval backdrop of the historic home of Antonio Stradivari.

Hell, if he couldn't win her over here in this romantic setting, he might as well give up trying.

A hand landed on his shoulder and he tensed, one hand groping beneath his sports jacket for the gun he hadn't carried in years.

He spun around, then relaxed when he saw his old friend and comrade-in-arms Hamish Gladstone standing behind him. With an exasperated laugh, Rocky jumped to his feet and gave Hamish a fist-clenching handshake and one-armed embrace. "Hamish! Didn't expect to see you here."

Hamish glanced around surreptitiously. "It's Amos this week," he said, his brogue as strong as ever. "Amos Ballantyne."

Rocky cocked an eyebrow. "Amos?"

"Yeah." Hamish's voice dropped. "Here on a story."

Hamish had put on a few pounds in the five years since Rocky had seen his old friend. His traditional Scottish tweeds, complete with vest, fit tight around his middle. He had grown a handlebar moustache too, possibly for this gig. Most noticeable though, was the dyed black hair, quite at odds with his red-head's complexion.

Rocky nodded. "Got it. So *Amos*, what are you doing here?"

"As you know, I've always been an amateur violinist," Hamish said, straight faced. "Now that I've made, well, to be frank, a killing in the tech sector, I thought I'd buy myself a good violin."

"Really. Tech sector," Rocky repeated, not blinking.

"Sold the business for a tidy profit," Hamish said evenly.

He was obviously deep in character, and before Rocky could react, his old friend settled on the stool next to him, casually raised an eyebrow and asked, "You?"

"Here covering the trade show and the competition," Rocky said. "And whatever other stories we can dig up this week."

Hamish nodded and downed the drink that looked glued to his hand.

"Just get into town?" Rocky asked. He was dying to know what Hamish was really doing here, but couldn't risk blowing his friend's cover by grilling him in such a public place.

They had both given up war zone reporting after a screwup in Aleppo five years ago where they had both nearly been killed. Since then, he had followed his old friend's career in print and online, and knew Hamish had switched battlefields. Now he had become quite the whistleblower, reporting on corruption in high places and digging up information that had sent more than one industry giant to jail. Rocky wondered what he could be digging into this week in this historic center of the violin world that was serious enough that he felt he needed to use an alias.

"I came in last week and have been talking to dealers around town." Hamish looked abashed. "I know I don't play well, it's really just a hobby, but I get a thrill out of holding these famous old instruments. I'm dying to add one to my collection."

Rocky nodded, hiding a smile. "Your collection. I'd love to see it."

Hamish tilted his head, squinting thoughtfully. One side of his face twitched, a quirk Rocky remembered that made Hamish look both sly and excited at the same time. "The violin world is a funny place. It's both international and very small at the same time."

"And that whole world will be here this week," Rocky added. Instrument makers, dealers and players were all meeting in Cremona for Mondo Musica, and if Hamish was here, Rocky just bet something big was going down.

Hamish gave him the sly look again. "This is always a lively town. Dealers and players all looking for the best instruments in the world – at the best prices. But this week we're bound to see more action than usual."

"I understand there are still about a hundred violin makers here," Rocky said, motioning to the bartender for two more of whatever Hamish was drinking.

Hamish nodded. "Lots of new violin makers, and deal-ers who mostly sell new instruments. But a few have old violins stashed away, too."

Rocky tilted his head. "Really old? Like the ones in the museum?"

Hamish tilted his head. "There's always the chance that one of the dealers might have a real Strad tucked away in their closet. I've heard there are usually one or two classic old instruments on offer – if you know where to look. And Stradivari wasn't the only important maker. There are other big names from the golden age, too. Rumor has it a fabulous old instrument, a Guarneri, recently surfaced after being lost for decades."

Rocky's eyes narrowed. "And that's what you're after."

Hamish's lifted one corner of his mouth in a hint of a smile. "I'm following a few leads."

The bartender appeared with their drinks. Scotch on the rocks. Hamish grabbed the tab and scribbled his room number – 301.

Rocky accepted his drink, tipping his head in thanks. "Hard to believe *any* instrument could have survived for three hundred years. It's amazing. They look so fragile."

Hamish gave him an enigmatic nod. "Amazing indeed."

"What does one go for?" Rocky asked, bringing his glass to his lips and taking a sip.

"Upwards of eighteen million."

Rocky choked, the harsh liquor burning a path down his throat. "Dollars?" he croaked.

"Pounds," Hamish said.

Chapter 4

B efore Rocky could respond to such a crazy valuation for a violin, Bernadette walked into the restaurant. She scanned the room with a slight frown, then saw him at the bar and her face lit up. He took another big sip of his Scotch and set the glass back on the counter.

Hamish followed his glance and his eyebrows rose enquiringly.

"My partner, Bernadette."

She looked bright and shiny, revived by her shower, her hair damp on her shoulders, the curling tendrils softening her pointy jaw. Her summer freckles were fading, and a warm flush brushed the tops of her otherwise pale cheeks.

Remembering Hamish's wolfish reputation with women, Rocky drew Bernadette to his side as she approached with a discreet hand on the small of her back.

Hamish sent him a knowing grin and stood to shake Bernadette's hand. "Amos Ballantyne. An old friend of Rocky's."

Bernadette took his hand, and through the thin fabric of her dress Rocky felt her back stiffen. Hamish didn't seem to notice, but Rocky wondered what she felt. A transfer of energy from Hamish's hand to her own? He knew that sometimes she sensed something when she shook a stranger's hand and, in Mexico, it never seemed to signal anything good.

But the moment passed as quickly as it happened, leaving him wondering if it had been anything at all.

He motioned to the bartender, then looked to Bernadette for her order.

"I don't know," she said with a grin. "Something Italian?"

"Campari with soda," Rocky suggested. Something light. She'd had a long day and he knew she didn't handle liquor well at the best of times. The bartender nodded and got busy mixing her drink.

"Rocky and I go way back," Hamish said, leaning heavily on the bar. He was rolling his r's like a Highland Lord, and Rocky realized this wasn't his old friend's second drink. Or probably even his third. "Had quite the time in the Middle East, didn't we, old man?"

Bernadette looked quizzically at Rocky. "I didn't know you spent time in the Middle East."

And he didn't plan to go into it now. "Never a dull moment when Amos is around."

"What are you doing in Cremona?" Bernadette asked.

Hamish pressed his lips together and shook his head. "Can't talk about it yet. But I'll tell you this, I'm on the trail of something big. Maybe the biggest lead of my career."

Rocky caught Bernadette's questioning look, but just shrugged one shoulder and reached for his drink. They couldn't talk here. Not in public. Not in the bar. It would have to wait until later.

Right then, four teenagers, an international mix, rolled into the restaurant and joined them at the bar. A young man settled on the seat next to Rocky. He looked Japanese but spoke to the other young people in English with an American accent, and then in passable Italian to the bartender.

"Time to get to work," Rocky said to Hamish under his breath.

"Me too," Hamish replied. He lifted his glass in a toast, drained it, set it heavily on the counter and walked away. Bernadette quickly claimed his seat, turning so she could see Rocky and into the room.

Rocky watched Hamish in the mirror above the bar as he drifted over to join two men already seated at a table. One had a fancy curled moustache and wore a shiny three-piece suit that fit tightly across his round belly. The other, a distinguished older gentleman with a long beard, wore a slightly shabby tweed jacket. They spoke in Italian and by the way they greeted the waiter by name, Rocky concluded they were probably local. And from the way the wait staff hovered around them, he guessed they must be influential men in town.

The men greeted Hamish affably as he approached – obviously not their first meeting – and offered him a seat. Rocky would have loved to join them and find out what story Hamish was really working on, but that would have to wait. He had his own job to do.

Turning to the young man beside him, he asked, "Are you here for the Cremona Crown Competition?"

The teen held out his hand to shake. "I am a contestant. Jay Takeuchi. I'm from the U.S." He gestured to his friends. "We're all in the competition."

This was a goldmine, a photographer's dream, a veritable United Nations of photogenic young people.

"I'm a photographer," Rocky said. "My partner and I are covering the competition. I would love to photograph all of you."

Jay's dark eyes lit up. "That would be great."

"Are you all traveling alone?" Bernadette asked.

"No. It's against contest rules," Jay responded with a wince. "We're all staying here in the hotel with our chaperones. Our parents or our teachers." He twitched, and Rocky could have sworn the pretty blonde on his other side gave him an elbow to the ribs, prompting him to say, "This is my teacher, Gloria Switzer."

The woman didn't look much older than Jay. It was hard to believe she was his chaperone. Rocky glanced at Bernadette and could tell by the difficulty she was having keeping her eyebrows in place that she thought so too.

They only had a few minutes to chat before the head-waiter motioned that Rocky and Bernadette's table was ready. As they stood up to go, Bernadette said, "We have tickets for the Crown concerts. I can't wait to hear you all play."

Rocky guided her with a hand on her back as they followed the waiter to their table. The restaurant was a dimly lit intimate space, where candles glowed and crystal glasses sparkled on tables spread with red damask cloths. Three walls and the ceiling were covered with intricately carved wooden paneling that added to the cozy, old-world ambiance. Their table was against the wall of windows that looked out onto the dark cobblestone street.

Once they'd taken their seats, another waiter approached.

"Sparkling mineral water okay to start?" Rocky asked Bernadette.

"Yes, thanks. I'm parched from the plane."

"*Aqua minerale, frizzante,*" Rocky ordered. After the waiter left, he turned to Bernadette and asked, "How's your room?"

She hesitated for a moment, then said, "Great."

"Is there a problem?"

"No. It's just – so modern. Still very Italian, but *new* Italian. I was hoping for something older."

Rocky laughed. "Just be glad the plumbing works. You'll see *old* Italian when we get to the farm."

"Your family's farm?"

Rocky nodded. "It's about five miles out of town. It's been in the family for hundreds of years. It's an organic dairy now. Cows and cheese."

Bernadette grinned. "Seriously?"

"It's fantastic cheese," Rocky insisted, then shrugged. "You'll see."

"Who lives there now?"

"My *zia* and *zio*. My aunt and uncle. We'll go out there soon and you can meet them."

Bernadette smiled. "I'd like that."

They ordered food and wine, and an hour later Rocky watched Bernadette savor the last bite of her *osso buco*, veal shanks in a delectable sauce of white wine, tomato paste and vegetables, as she scraped the remaining sauce off her plate. He liked watching her eat. She loved to eat and wasn't afraid to show it.

When she finished, she sat back and sighed deeply. "That was fantastic."

"Pretty good for restaurant food," he agreed. "But wait until you taste my Zia Sophia's cooking. I spent a year with them on the farm a while ago. Before I got my first photography job." Thankfully, the memory of that traumatic year after he'd left the police force and San Francisco was fading. He credited Zia Sophia's cooking and the demanding work on the farm with bringing him back to the land of the living.

"And who was that job for?" Bernadette asked.

"*News of the World* magazine."

Bernadette frowned. "That covers hard-core political issues, doesn't it?"

"I guess," Rocky said, trying to keep it deliberately vague.

"Is that when you went to the Middle East?"

He gave a brief nod. And here they were again, talking about his work with Hamish in Syria. Time to change the subject. He raised a hand, trying to catch the waiter's eye.

Bernadette took the hint and, sitting back with her wine glass in her hand, said, "I'd like to visit your family's farm. On my first trip to Italy years ago I only went to the archeological dig I was on and into the small town nearby, but the old farmhouses I saw from the train really caught my imagination."

"It is pretty cool, but not that romantic when you have to muck out the stalls. We'll make time, but we do have a busy week ahead."

"I know. This time I was able to do some research."

Rocky knew that before their Mexico trip the previous spring, she did not have enough time to prepare. He had given her grief about her lack of experience, but she had come through in the end. Despite the distractions on the trip, they managed to hand in quality stories to *Let's Travel* and several other magazines and online e-zines.

He looked at her across the table. "I think this trip will be different. I think we'll have fun."

Her cheeks flushed and she took a sip of her drink. "I hope so."

A woman in a fuchsia coat entered the restaurant trailing a fragile, young-looking girl. The woman's gaze swept the room, then they joined the table of contestants Rocky and Bernadette had met at the bar.

Bernadette was watching the contestants' table too. "I studied the violin for a while," she said. "But I had never heard of Cremona before."

"How long did you play?"

"Just a few years. As a child."

Knowing her upbringing, he should have suspected. "How many years, exactly?"

She glanced away, then picked up her glass again. "Twelve."

"Twelve? You must be good."

She shook her head. "I hardly play at all anymore. One of the things that fell by the wayside when I had Colin."

Rocky picked up his wine glass and sat back in his chair. "So, how is your son?"

Her face lit up. "Growing like a weed."

"Still playing soccer?"

She nodded. "You bet."

While they'd been eating, Rocky had been keeping an eye on a burly man sitting alone at a table with his back to the wall. Now the man stood and motioned for his bill. From the way he had been surveying the room, with particular interest in Hamish's table, Rocky had him pegged as police. He wondered what the man found so interesting, Hamish, or the other men at his table?

The man signed for his bill and on his way to the door, stopped at Hamish's table. He put a hand on the shoulder of the bearded man, said a few words, bid everyone goodnight, then walked out into the lobby. Rocky tucked that interesting tidbit away and tuned back in to what Bernadette was saying.

"Cremona sounds like an amazing town. I can't wait to see the square."

"The square is pretty spectacular," he admitted. "Especially at night. Feel like a little walk? It's just around the corner."

Bernadette's face lit up. "Just let me finish my wine."

Chapter 5

I t might have been the food, or the wine, or maybe the company, but whatever the reason, Bernadette found her second wind over dinner. She glanced at her watch – nine o'clock – and couldn't help calculating what time it would be at home. *Noon?* She had been up all night on the plane, so she'd been awake for what? Twenty-four hours? She never could figure out time zone differences, only knew she wasn't sleepy anymore. A bit of night air might help her sleep better and wake up tomorrow morning on Cremona time.

For this assignment, she'd had three weeks warning before the trip and had gone full out on research, hoping to wipe away any memory Rocky might have of her pitifully unprofessional start to their first assignment together in Mexico.

"I'm also looking forward to visiting the Stradivarius Museum," she said as Rocky signaled the waiter for the bill.

"Ah, yes. Strad and his pals. The golden age of violin making. There was a whole community of violin makers in

Cremona and Brescia in the late sixteen hundreds. Some of them are almost as famous as he is. At least to violinists."

"Over one hundred luthiers still live in Cremona," Bernadette said excitedly. "I hope we can arrange to talk to a few."

"My cousin Mia is apprenticing with one of the old masters," Rocky said. "I'll ask her to set up a meeting for us. They'll all be busy at Mondo Musica this weekend, but hopefully we can line up interviews for after the show."

The waiter arrived, they signed for their bills and Rocky said, "Let's take that walk."

Outside it was cooler than when they'd arrived. The autumn days were too short for the heat of the afternoon sun to penetrate the pavement and medieval stone walls flanking the street. Bernadette shivered, crossed her arms on her chest, and was reconsidering the idea of a walk when Rocky peeled off his light wool jacket and draped it over her shoulders. "We won't go far."

Bernadette pulled the garment close, savoring his warmth and the light woodsy scent of aftershave that clung to the fabric.

Half a block away, the cathedral glowed at the end of the narrow street. When they stepped out of the side street and onto the piazza, Bernadette paused, transfixed by the sight. Ambient light from hidden fixtures played across the facades of the ancient buildings surrounding the square, highlighting the art and geometry of architecture that spanned centuries, from medieval to Renaissance times. The cathedral was the focal point of the cobblestoned square, a benevolent presence whose giant stained-glass rose window glowed with medieval magic.

Rocky pulled out his camera and took a few shots. "The Cathedral of Santa Maria Assunta. They call it the *Duomo.*"

In the midst of all this beauty, Bernadette felt her shoulders relax. She took a deep breath and slowly let it out. It was beginning to sink in. She really was in Italy.

They strolled past an octagonal, Romanesque building that Rocky identified as the Baptistry, the oldest building in the town center, then stopped for a moment to admire the primitive stone lions flanking the steps of the Duomo. Next to the cathedral, the tower, *Il Torrazzo,* presided like a concerned parent over the venerable square.

This was clearly the heart of the ancient city. Eight cobble-stone streets ran into the square like spokes of a wheel. From their size, Bernadette guessed they were primarily pedestrian. The dim, empty side streets looked enticing as they circled past, but she was too cold to want to explore tonight. She pulled Rocky's jacket closer as they rounded the final corner of the square and entered the covered colonnade of the *Loggia dei Militi,* built, Rocky told her, in 1292.

It was darker under the arches of the colonnade, and the cold seemed more intense. The row of columns holding up the roof cast diagonal shadows across a stone floor worn smooth by centuries of foot traffic.

Suddenly Bernadette felt a cold fog creep up her legs. It seeped out of the chilled flagstones and circled her body. Her teeth began to chatter and she started to shake.

Panic engulfed her. *Not here. Not now*!

Her head spun and, fighting to control her pounding heart, she tried to hold on to the sensation as her consciousness began to slip away. She put out a hand to steady herself, relieved to feel the solid, cold stone wall beside her.

She'd experienced these premonitions before, but so rarely that she had never learned to control them or to interpret them clearly. One thing she did know – they usually meant trouble.

Her Grandmother Bernadette had told her to ride the wave, try to absorb the feelings. But try as she might, that always seemed impossible, and now the vapor continued to roll around her until even Rocky disappeared.

A faint, melancholy line of music like that of a single violin wound through the mist, the melody vaguely familiar, but she couldn't put her finger on the name of the piece.

Then suddenly the fog dissipated, as quickly and quietly as it had rolled in, and as usual, the feeling began to fade before she could fully grasp its meaning. She blew out a breath and opened her eyes to find Rocky holding her arm, his gaze intent.

"Damn you!" she said, only half joking, pulling away her arm and rubbing a hand across her forehead.

His eyebrows rose. "What do I have to do with it?"

She was glad to see that when he witnessed her spells, he wasn't as freaked out as most people were – first and foremost her mother and father.

"I have been perfectly all right at home for the past six months. Not a shiver or a peep since Mexico. It must be you."

He took her hand and led her out of the colonnade into the open, cobbled square. She was relieved to feel the ground solid beneath her feet but glanced back over her shoulder as they walked to the side street that led to their hotel.

"I'm sure it's nothing," she said briskly, pulling her hand away. "Probably just a dead cat."

"My Aunt Sophia would say a dead cat was a bad omen," Rocky said, and although one corner of his mouth tugged up in a grin, Bernadette suspected he thought his aunt might be right.

And, she had to admit, so did she.

Chapter 6

Without further discussion, they headed back to the hotel. Bernadette excused herself to go to the washroom, and Rocky went into the bar and ordered a glass of wine.

He could tell that the spell – or attack or whatever you wanted to call it – in the square had left her shaken. He frowned as he replayed it in his mind. It only lasted a few seconds. She stopped, her eyes fluttered briefly, then closed for a fleeting moment. She put out a hand to steady herself on the colonnade wall, and then it was over. If he hadn't been right there beside her, looking right at her, he would have missed it.

She said it was nothing, but when it happened in Mexico, it had foreshadowed seriously nefarious activities taking place right in their hotel. Activities that, before the week ended, had put her life in jeopardy.

He hoped this time it *was* just a dead cat because he'd been looking forward to an uneventful, easygoing week, working, visiting relatives, and getting to know his new partner better. He had already been in Italy for a week and had become acclimatized – in body and mind. And, he reflected as he enjoyed another sip of his earthy *primitivo* wine, even in spirit.

The moment he landed on Italian soil, he felt himself slow down and unwind. Although he had only lived here for ten months five years ago, it felt like coming home. When he was here, even the *pausa*, the rest Italians took after lunch, felt right. It was something he would never do at home, but here he stayed up later, got up earlier, drank more wine, and talked and laughed more freely. Everything felt slightly more real, or maybe he just felt everything more intensely. There was a lot to be said for the Italian way of life. Of course, the tangle of bureaucracy made some things take longer to happen, but in his present state of mind, he didn't really care.

Bernadette had seemed distant at the airport, making him wonder if he had imagined the connection they had developed in Mexico. But she had gotten her second wind and at dinner was her old self. A smile quirked the corner of his mouth. The woman liked to eat. He'd have to get her out to the *azienda familiare* and have his aunt Sophia prepare her a real Italian meal.

A brittle, tinkling laugh broke into his thoughts, and from his seat at the bar he saw members of the Cremona Crown party still scattered in small groups around the restaurant. The woman in the fuchsia coat and the man she had been sitting beside at dinner had taken a private table in the back corner, but Rocky couldn't see any sign of her fragile looking protégé. Jay, the American kid, and his attractive companion were the only ones left at the big table. She might be his teacher, but it was hard to believe she was his chaperone, not the way he leaned over her, one hand draped possessively on the back of her chair. She might be ten years older than Jay, but she hung on his every word as if their roles were reversed.

Out of the corner of his eye, Rocky saw the woman in the bright pink coat stand up, loudly say good night to her companion and head out through the lobby alone, turning toward the exit rather than the elevators. Rocky wondered where she was going at this time of night. She was one of the Crown contestant chaperones, and Jay had said all of the contestants were staying in the hotel, but this week people were getting together in bars and restaurants all around town. Places he knew nothing about.

Hamish and his men friends were sitting back enjoying a *digestivo*, a traditional after-dinner drink. Speaking surprisingly fluent Italian, Hamish raised his glass in a toast that brought roars of laughter from the other two men. Rocky would have given a bottle of his favorite Brunello to know what they were talking about.

Bernadette appeared at his side, startling him out of his reverie. "Penny for your thoughts?" she said, slipping onto the stool beside him.

He shook his head and smiled. "Just thinking how glad I am to be here."

Hamish pulled himself away from the group at the table, shaking both men's hands and patting their shoulders, and made his way over to where Rocky and Bernadette sat at the bar.

Rocky raised his glass. "Time for one more?" He was dying to find out what his old friend was up to here in this quiet, violin-making town.

Hamish laid a hand on his shoulder. "Rain check?"

Rocky glanced at the watch on his friend's wrist, a Breitling Bentley that must have set him back more than ten grand. Clearly Hamish was playing the part of a big spender so he had to dress the part but, knowing Hamish, the watch was likely borrowed.

"I have to meet someone in a few minutes," he said.

It was almost midnight, but Rocky knew that here in Cremona during the week of Mondo Musica deals would be made at all hours, all over town. The other two men from Hamish's table headed out the door, acknowledging him with a wave and a word as they passed the bar.

As they walked out the door, Rocky asked, "Who are your friends?"

Hamish jingled the change in his pocket and glanced over his shoulder, watching as the men exited through the lobby. Neither seemed to be staying at the hotel, adding credence to Rocky's notion that they were locals.

"The guy with the moustache is Alessandro Fanucci, a big dealer in town. No really good instruments go through Cremona without undergoing his inspection first. And the man with the beard is Marco Passero. He's local, Italian. One of the violin-making competition judges."

Passero. Rocky remembered that was the name of his cousin Mia's boss.

Hamish glanced at his watch again. "Got to go. See you later and we'll catch up." He nodded, including Bernadette, before hurrying out the door.

"Wonder where's he off to?" Rocky murmured softly, watching through the leaded window as Hamish stopped on the street outside and spoke again to the older man with the long white beard who had been sitting at his table.

Passero glanced back down the dark street as they spoke. Hamish put a reassuring hand on the older man's shoulder, then, as Passero hurried away, Hamish started down the narrow street in the opposite direction, toward the Duomo Piazza.

"Isn't Amos staying here at the hotel?" Bernadette asked.

"He is. He signed for a drink."

"Late to be heading out," she commented.

Rocky grinned. "This is Italy. The night is still young."

Bernadette yawned. "Not for me. We have a busy day tomorrow."

She started to list the events they planned to cover, but Rocky was only half listening. He was still thinking about Hamish's mysterious business when, in the distance, a faint pop, or the echo of a pop, caught his attention. A memory triggered deep in his sub-conscious. He'd know the sound of a gunshot anywhere.

Bernadette was still talking as Rocky threw some euros on the bar and stood up.

Her brows furrowed in a frown. "What's up?"

"Not sure. Stay here."

He hurried to the door, through the lobby and stepped outside. The street was dark and empty. He pulled up his jacket collar. The temperature had dropped, but it was the fear of what he would find in the square that chilled him to the bone.

Bernadette stepped out of the lobby and stood shivering beside him. He should have known she wouldn't stay put.

"Come on," he said, and as they headed toward the glow of cathedral square, he had to admit he was glad she was there.

Chapter 7

In the deserted piazza, the cold evening air raised an eerie mist from the warm, damp ground, muting the light of the Duomo rose window.

The square was silent and empty, except for a figure sprawled in the shadow of the colonnade, a trail of blood dripping off the stone step onto the cobbles of the square.

Rocky's gut clenched. He glanced over his shoulder to make sure they were alone, then hurried to the body. *Hamish.* His heart sank.

He knelt beside his old friend and pressed his fingers to the pulse point at his neck. He was still warm, but there was no reassuring beat. Hamish had followed one lead too many.

Rocky knelt for a moment beside Hamish's body, weighing his options. He owed this man his life, but it was too late now to return the favor.

He stood and turned to Bernadette. "He's dead."

She gasped and put a hand to her mouth.

He pulled out his phone and dialed 112. When the emergency operator answered he said, "C'è stato un morto in Piazza Duomo." Then he ended the call.

They shouldn't hang around. He took Bernadette's hand and pulled her toward the hotel. "Come on."

She dug in her heels. "Shouldn't we stay?"

"Best not to be found hovering over the body, the only people at the scene."

In the distance, a siren wailed.

"Anyway," he added. "At this point, we don't know anything that would help." He gave her arm a little tug.

Reluctantly, she followed. "I guess not. If he's already dead."

"He's dead all right," Rocky said through clenched teeth.

The sirens grew louder, echoing through the stone corridors of the town, making it hard to tell from which direction they were coming.

Rocky and Bernadette turned the corner and stepped into the shadow of their hotel. Seconds later, the swirling lights of police cars lit up the square behind them.

Once inside the hotel, Bernadette headed straight to the elevators. "I'm going to bed."

Rocky followed her. "Are you okay?"

She gave a shrill little laugh as she pushed the up button. "Okay? I don't think so." Then she shook her head and seemed to pull herself together. "You're right. We have to let the police handle it. I'll be okay. I'm just going to go to bed."

She looked small and fragile in the harsh light of the hotel lobby, so Rocky took her by the shoulders and pulled her in for a hug. She was stiff, but after a moment, slumped against him. When the elevator doors whooshed open, he gave her a quick kiss on the forehead, as you would a child who awoke from a nightmare, and let her go.

"I'll be up in a few minutes," he said.

She nodded and got into the elevator. When the doors closed, he turned abruptly toward the bar.

He didn't usually drink hard liquor, but this time he ordered a single malt Scotch. When it arrived, he raised the glass in a silent toast to Hamish, then drank. His shoulders twitched as the warmth ran through him, chasing the chill in his bones. He sat for a while, contemplating his choices: his need to find the person who had killed his friend, and his instinct to stay out of the investigation.

Finally, his decision was made. This was Cremona, and in Italy things had a habit of becoming complicated. He'd let the police manage it. The last thing he wanted was to be pulled into whatever scheme Hamish had planned, especially one that had gotten him murdered.

Wednesday, Day Two

Chapter 8

Rocky hardly slept that night. The image of his old friend lying dead on the cold stones kept flashing before his eyes. His feverish brain imagined one scenario after another of what might have happened in the few minutes between the time they'd said goodbye in the hotel bar, and when he and Bernadette found Hamish dead in the square.

In the end he decided, for the umpteenth time, that this was Italy, he didn't know anything, and it wouldn't do any good to get involved. Better to let the police handle it and stick to the original plan of getting their story for the magazine.

But the acid roiling in his gut refused to give him peace. Finally at seven in the morning, when he thought the restaurant would be open for business, he made his way downstairs to the bar.

The espresso machine was steaming and the barista had laid out a light self-serve breakfast, but the room was empty, so he sat at a table by the window. Moments later a mother and daughter pair he'd seen at the Cremona

Crown table the night before came in. The mother flashed Rocky an openly seductive smile. "Mind if we join you?"

Rocky sighed, reminding himself he had a job to do. "Of course."

The woman was probably pushing fifty. Her milky complexion as well as her accent suggested she was British. She held out a hand dangerously full of diamonds to Rocky. He shook off thoughts of the murder and automatically turned on the charm. To ensure good photographs, it was essential he make friends with the people involved. He smiled at the woman and took her hand, cold and bony and heavy with stones.

"Hello. You must be one of the reporters," she said. "I am Agatha Frost, and this is my daughter Cordelia." She didn't glance at her daughter during the introduction, but Cordelia, a flushed-faced girl with kinky, strawberry blonde curls, held up her hand in a wave.

"Rocky Falconi. I'm working on a story about the competition with my partner Bernadette Mallow. It's nice to meet you. And you, Cordelia."

Cordelia giggled, her face flushing salmon red.

Agatha's eyes brightened and she sat up taller. "Are you writing about the contestants? Perhaps we might set up a time for an interview?" Although Cordelia might be the talent, Agatha was obviously the driving force in her daughter's career. Until he knew if Cordelia would be one of the front runners in the competition, he didn't want to get wrapped in Agatha's tentacles. He had a feeling that once that happened, she wouldn't let go.

Rocky sidestepped the offer with a charming smile. "Like I said, I'm a photographer. My partner Bernadette is the writer."

Suddenly the dark-haired woman in the bright pink coat appeared in the doorway, stopping on the step to haughtily survey the room. Her pale charge waited silently behind her.

"Who is that woman?" Rocky quietly asked Agatha as the diva swept into the room. "I couldn't help noticing her at dinner last night."

Agatha leaned forward, her low-cut blouse revealing a little too much cleavage for so early in the morning. She lowered her voice conspiratorially and her accent deepened, obviously happy to spread a little gossip. "That's Mirela Florescu. She's the Romanian girl's coach. Mirela used to be a violinist herself, but wasn't talented enough to really get anywhere. Now she coaches Tatiana." She leaned in closer. "That girl is *very* talented, and if Mirela would just back off, Tatiana would be a real contender for the Crown." She sat back with a dramatic sigh. "But I'm afraid Mirela stifles the girl dreadfully."

Cordelia, her face fading back to freckles in milk, leaned past her mother and added eagerly, "Tatiana looked sickly at the European trials last month, but now she looks positively ghastly!"

Cordelia's tone was almost gleeful, although Rocky agreed with her assessment. His mind went back to Mirela. Hard to see how bullying would build Tatiana's confidence for competition.

"Has she been coaching Tatiana for long?"

"Mirela just started as Tatiana's coach when Tat won her spot in this competition," Cordelia said.

"I wonder how she managed that?" Rocky mused.

Agatha was more than happy to enlighten him. "Mirela was here fifteen years ago – as a competitor."

"She was that good?" Rocky asked.

Jay Takeuchi slid into the seat on his other side and responded bluntly, "She didn't win."

Rocky raised his brows. "Surely just getting here is an honor."

Jay cut him off with a humorless laugh. "Right. Like they say at the Oscars. That's a bunch of bullshit."

His teacher Gloria trailed in behind him and she pushed out her full lips in an attractive pout at his language. He responded with a challenging look from his far-from-innocent eyes. Then he shrugged. "It's all or nothing."

"What's the prize?" Rocky asked.

Cordelia giggled childishly. "A violin. The winning violin from the instrument competition at Mondo Musica this week. We won't know which violin it will be until the end of the instrument judging, the same day as the Crown finale."

"Nice," Agatha said dismissively. "But we'd sell it. A new and untried violin will not compete with Cordelia's Amati."

Gloria leaned forward to catch Rocky's eye. "The violin is just part of it. What's important is the publicity that goes with the title."

Jay nodded. "You can tour for two years on the prestige of winning the Crown." His eyes glazed over and he stared into the distance as if visualizing himself on the world stage.

Rocky looked at him thoughtfully and wondered to what lengths the young man was willing to go for an opportunity like that.

Chapter 9

Bernadette woke that morning to the somber toll of cathedral bells. Even before she opened her eyes, the bells reminded her she was in Italy. Her residual jetlag cleared surprisingly quickly and she jumped out of bed.

The night before, she'd lain awake for hours, battling the time change and reliving the discovery of Amos's body. Because, let's face it, after the psychic episode in the square, she'd felt that something bad was coming. As usual, though, she hadn't known exactly what.

She felt helpless after finding the body, and frustrated that she hadn't been able to prevent his death. That she hadn't warned him. Because, thinking back, when they'd first shaken hands she had felt a little charge, but at the time she had put it down to his flirtatious gaze.

At some point in the night she must have fallen asleep, and now the time zone changes were clicking in and she was starving.

She hurried to dress and fifteen minutes later strolled into the hotel restaurant. Rocky was already seated at a table with two women, a tiny espresso cup empty before him and the remains of a flaky pastry littering his plate.

He looked like he hadn't slept much either, dark shadows creeping under his deep brown eyes.

Bernadette dropped into the chair across from him, and greeted the women sitting at the table, whom he introduced as the British contestants, and Jay and Gloria whom she'd met the night before. Then she said, "I need coffee."

"The waiter will bring you coffee, but the complimentary breakfast – and I say that in quotes – is self-serve," Rocky told her.

At that moment, the waiter appeared, and Bernadette ordered a cappuccino. Then, following Rocky's instructive point toward a table in the corner, she got up and examined the feeble display of store-bought pastries, still in their original cellophane wrappers.

When she returned to her seat, she was glad to see that the Crown contestants had moved to sit with their fellows at a larger table. Bernadette took the first long sip of the glorious hot coffee and sighed. She watched Rocky across the table over the rim of her cup. He seemed preoccupied. She was sure the murder was weighing on his mind, but before she could comment, a high-pitched British voice behind her asked loudly, "Did you hear about the murder?"

Bernadette's cup clattered against the saucer as she set it down. Her gaze locked with Rocky's. He pressed his lips together and gave a tight shake of his head.

"Nothing to do with us," he murmured. "Finish up. We have to meet my cousin Paola. She's giving us a ride to my aunt and uncle's farm. My uncle is lending us a car."

Bernadette was a little surprised that Rocky didn't feel any impulse to get involved with the investigation into

Amos's death. They were, after all, old friends. But she was beginning to notice a pattern in his behavior consistent with his actions on their first trip. He seemed to try his hardest not to get involved in local problems. And he was probably right. This might not be the time or place to announce their connection to the dead man.

Someone at another table asked, "Who was it?"

The British voice answered. "No one knows! The police were in the square this morning and our waiter told Angelo there was a murder."

The store-bought pastry had been unappetizing to begin with, but now turned to cardboard in Bernadette's mouth.

Rocky glanced over his shoulder at the other table then nodded at her cup. "Finish your coffee."

Her eyes narrowed as she recalled his annoying habit of issuing orders. But this morning he was justifiably stressed, so she decided to choose her battles. She downed her cappuccino, gathered her things together, and followed him in silence out of the hotel .

Once on the street, though, she couldn't restrain herself. "We have to tell someone."

Rocky took her arm and turned her toward the Cathedral. "They already know. You heard the sirens. We don't want to get involved. I'll tell the police what I know, but only when they ask. If they ask. And really, I don't know anything. Anyway, right now we have to get the car."

Unlike the silence of the previous evening, the Piazza Duomo was buzzing with activity. A police car was parked beside the area where they had found Hamish's body the night before and a yellow tape cordoned off the arches of the portico. Two police men lounged against a pillar, casually surveying the crowd as people stopped to speculate about what might have happened.

They turned onto one of the narrow streets off the square, which soon opened onto another tree-filled square that Rocky called Piazza Roma. The streets around this square were lined with venerable buildings, their ground floor store windows filled with the latest in fashion and home décor from Milan. The displays were an incongruous contrast to the earth-toned stucco of the upper floors, where patches of the original red brick, hundreds of years old, peeked through breaks in the ochre and sienna plaster.

People in business suits hurried in and out of tiny coffee bars tucked in ancient storefronts that the previous evening had been shuttered and barred. Most were unaware that a murder had taken place in the piazza only one block away. Students in school uniforms whizzed by on bicycles and small children heading to school tugged on their mothers' hands.

As they walked into the tree-filled square, Bernadette asked, "What kind of work do people here do?"

"Cremona is the provincial capital so there are a lot of banking and administrative jobs." Rocky laughed. "Italians love administration. You have to fill out a million forms to get any real work done.

"The main industry is still violin making though," he continued. "It's made the city tick for hundreds of years, since the seventeenth and eighteenth centuries, the time of Stradivari, Amati, and the Guarneri family. Violin making almost died out for a while, but Mussolini resurrected the art in the 1930's when he opened the *Scuola di Violini de*

Cremona. After the war, the school brought in students from around the world. Now there are two schools and over one hundred violin makers in Cremona again, most of them Italian."

At the edge of the park, they crossed the road and stopped in front of a storefront window that featured violins. In fact, now that Bernadette really looked, it seemed every storefront, regardless of what it sold, was celebrating the annual festival with an instrument worked into the display. Even the lingerie store window had two violins, crossed at the necks, with ruby red thongs and lacy bras draped salaciously over them. Bernadette turned to Rocky and raised one skeptical brow.

He grinned and indicated an actual violin maker's workshop two doors down. "*This* is where we're going."

Chapter 10

The word 'Passero' was painted in bold script on the large plate glass window, but no violins were displayed on the walls. Inside the shop, a young woman was packing violin cases into a large box on the floor.

Rocky stuck his head in through the doorway and called, "Ciao, Mia."

The woman looked up and smiled. She hurried over and gave Rocky a resounding double cheeked kiss, then finished her greeting with a cheerful tongue lashing in rapid-fire Italian.

"I know, I know," he said sheepishly in English. "I should have come by sooner."

The woman put her hands on her hips. "Yes, you should."

He put a hand on Bernadette's lower back to include her in the conversation. "This is my partner, Bernadette. My cousin Mia. She works for Maestro Passero."

Mia shook Bernadette's hand with a friendly smile. Then she turned back to Rocky and scolded, "Why did you wait? Now I am busy all weekend at Mondo Musica."

"You have a booth?" Rocky asked.

Mia nodded. "*Certo*. Of course. The shop has a big booth, and we must get all these violins set up by tonight for the grand opening."

An old man with a grizzled beard and sharp, if watery, blue eyes shuffled into the room carrying more violin cases. Bernadette recognized him as one of the men at the table with Amos the night before. She glanced at Rocky, but he didn't show any signs of recognition.

Passero frowned pointedly at Mia, who called to him, "*Signore Passero*, come and meet my cousin, the American journalist. He and his partner are writing a story about Cremona and the violin masters here. They would love to write about you and your shop."

Rocky gave her a quick, appreciative smile as Passero put down his load and came forward to shake hands. Instead of being happy at the thought of free publicity, however, the maestro seemed apprehensive. "Journalists? What do you want with me?"

Bernadette took his outstretched hand and smiled. "We are writing a travel article about Cremona and would love to have the opportunity to interview one of Italy's most famous violin makers."

Rocky thought she was laying it on a bit thick but at her words Passero relaxed. "Perhaps after Mondo Musica we will find some time."

"Bernadette is the writer," Rocky said. "I am a photographer. Would it be possible for me to photograph your shop, possibly with you at work?"

Passero nodded. "*Certamente*. But not now." He looked pointedly at the pile of open boxes in the center of the shop.

"I see you are busy," Rocky said smoothly. "Maybe we will see you at Mondo Musica."

Passero nodded and mumbled, "*Molto bene*," as he headed toward the back of the shop with one last pointed look at Mia.

"We'll leave you to it," Rocky said to Mia, turning to leave.

At the door, she gave him another kiss on the cheek, slipping two participant passes for the show into his hand. "These will help you get in," she said, then hurried back inside.

"That's a good contact," Bernadette said excitedly as they followed a trail of teenagers on bicycles down a cobbled side street.

Rocky nodded. "Any of the makers would be happy for the publicity, but I'd like to include Passero if possible because he is one of the old masters."

The group of cyclists they'd been following swung off through an arched entrance into a narrow stone passageway, but Rocky continued straight down the street.

Bernadette glanced at him. "I saw Passero last night. Twice. At dinner, then talking to Amos outside the bar."

Rocky nodded. "I noticed that too. He might have been the last person to speak to Amos before he died."

"I wonder what they were talking about," Bernadette mused.

They walked in silence for a few blocks down a wide street lined with neat, mid-century apartments, then suddenly Rocky said, "His name is Hamish."

Bernadette darted him a glance. "Who's name is Hamish?"

"My friend Amos. His real name is Hamish Gladstone."

Bernadette stopped in the middle of the sidewalk. "Why was he calling himself Amos?"

Rocky stopped as well. "He was undercover."

"A cop?"

"A reporter."

Bernadette mulled that over for a moment. "What was he investigating?"

Rocky started walking again. "I don't know."

Bernadette hurried to catch up. "What could have been that important – that *dangerous* – that it would get him killed?"

"Hamish had a nasty habit of blowing whistles on important people. People with something to hide."

Bernadette shook her head, confounded. "But this is Cremona, not Rome, or Milan, or, God forbid, Sicily."

Rocky shrugged one shoulder. "There are people with secrets everywhere. Even here."

Bernadette stopped again, her eyes wide with excitement. "And you're going to find out who it was."

Rocky didn't stop, just continued walking briskly down the street, forcing her to once again jog to catch up. "We are going to try to keep out of it, as much as possible. You don't know how the system here works."

"And you do."

"More than you. The Italian police system is terribly complicated." He shook his head. "Too many layers to unravel. I wouldn't want to get tangled up in any of it."

"You never do," Bernadette muttered.

Rocky glanced her direction and frowned. "What do you mean by that?"

Bernadette hitched her shoulders noncommittally. "Just that you said the same thing in Mexico –"

"With good reason –"

"– until we had no other choice."

"Yes, well this time we do have a choice, and I choose to let the police handle it."

They walked in silence for a few minutes, then she said, "He was killed right where I heard the music."

This time it was Rocky who stopped and turned toward her. "What music?"

"I didn't get a chance to tell you, but that was what happened when we were walking in the square after supper last night. When we were under the colonnade I heard a line of music... And before that, when I shook his hand in the bar I got a little charge, a feeling that something was – off."

Rocky nodded. "I thought you might have."

They started walking again. "Off," she stressed, "but not murder. I wonder what he was investigating."

"Hamish is – was – always stirring up trouble, and this time I guess he went too far. He said he was onto a big story, probably after someone, but that's all I know."

"And you're not going to look into it."

"No, I'm not."

"But he was your friend."

Rocky pressed his lips firmly together. "He was more than a friend. I owed him my life."

Chapter 11

When they were in Mexico, Bernadette had learned that Rocky did not like to talk about his past. So, although she had questions about why Rocky owed Hamish his life, she decided to let it go. For now.

They entered a park of poplars and scrubby brush and when the path turned a corner, they were suddenly at the bank of the Po River. A wide waterway, it flowed out of the Italian alps in the west, gathering volume as it crossed the fertile Po Valley, then emptied into the Adriatic Sea just south of Venice. Just downstream from where they stood, a large bridge spanned the wide, swiftly moving river. Below them, a bristle of wharves stuck out into the flow. Most looked like small private docks, but two were gated with long walkways leading to landing stages piled with row boats. A larger wharf at the end of the row boasted a small building that looked like it could have an official purpose.

"Where exactly are we meeting your cousin?"

"Here. There she is." A woman in jeans, a tee-shirt and rubber boots waved to them from where a boat was tied to one of the small docks. Rocky held up his hand to return the greeting.

Bernadette brightened. "We're going by boat?"

Rocky nodded and turned onto a rough path that led down the steep, rocky bank to the shore. A barge piled high with crates moved quickly past them down the dark, swollen river. "Farmers still use the Po to get produce to market," Rocky said. "This valley produces a lot of the food Italians eat."

They walked out on the dock, and Rocky exchanged light, double-cheek kisses with his cousin. After a quick, animated discussion in Italian, she turned to Bernadette, who managed a hasty, "*Ciao,*" as she did her best to field more air kisses.

Paola held a rope attached to a motorboat. It was a long, broad vessel with a wooden deck in front of a windscreen. Although there were padded seats for the driver and one passenger in the front and wooden bench seats along the sides in back, the launch looked more like a cargo boat than a passenger vessel.

As they clambered onboard, Bernadette asked, "Is your farm on the river?"

"*Si,*" Paola answered. "Is an old farm with river access, on an island down-river." She settled into the driver's seat, turned the key and the motor started with a noxious belch of blue-grey smoke. Rocky indicated Bernadette should take the passenger seat while he up-turned a bucket and sat between them.

The noise of the motor halted further conversation, so Bernadette settled in to enjoy this surprise river cruise. She dug her pad out of her bag and made notes as they slipped under the big steel bridge that spanned the broad river. Once past the edge of the city, Paola let out the throttle.

The sun was burning off the mist and sparkled droplets of spray that flew past. On the near bank, the river encroached on a mixture of mature trees that lined the shore. Sunlight shone through, softening tendrils of mist off the water. Soon the forest gave way to a pastoral scene, with low-lying fog spreading beyond the riverbanks, drifting across long fields divided by hedgerows. On the far side of the river, a raised dike followed the shore and on top of it, people rode bicycles toward town.

Rocky noticed the direction of her gaze and shouted over the noise of the motor. "The Po drains all of northern Italy. In the spring it can get high enough to reach the top of those dikes."

So, the river had a wild side. Looking into its depths, Bernadette sensed the latent power garnered from its rush down the slopes from the alps. The dike following the far shore suddenly swooped away from the riverbank and a green field took its place, a line of brown cows swaying towards the muddy shore.

Except for the raised dike, the land on either side of the river was flat. In some places brush crowded the shoreline and in others Bernadette saw fields and trees with the odd farm building, but nothing that looked like a farmhouse. If the river had a reputation of flooding, she could see why farmers built a safe distance back from its unpredictable banks.

Fifteen minutes later, Paola kicked back the throttle and brought them up slowly beside a sturdy dock. They all climbed out of the boat, but when Rocky and Bernadette headed to shore, Paola lagged behind, tying up. A battered scooter leaned against a post and Bernadette was suddenly mortified to realize that this was what the discussion on the dock in Cremona must have been about. Paola hadn't been expecting her.

"Is all right," Paola said, coming up beside them and brushing aside the problem of fitting three on the bike. "If I get back too soon I will just have to clean out the barn. I can walk. It's not far."

Bernadette was ready to refuse the suggestion and offer to walk herself, but Rocky gave Paola a quick peck on the cheek and climbed onto the small scooter, indicating Bernadette should climb on behind.

Giving up her attempt to be gracious, she threw her shoulder bag onto her back and straddled the seat. He gunned the motor and they shot off down the hard-packed dirt road, Bernadette holding onto Rocky with one arm, the other hand holding onto her hat.

Chapter 12

Bernadette clung to Rocky's back as the scooter bounced down the dirt road in a straight line through fields of stubble, the remains of the summer's crops of corn and hay. The fog had burned off and the sun shone fiercely down.

Peering over Rocky's shoulder, she watched as the farm buildings in the distance grew larger. Soon they rounded the corner of a red brick building and skidded to a stop.

Bernadette's eyes widened. It wasn't like any farm she'd ever seen. The buildings looked ancient and formed three sides of a large, dusty square with a crumbling stone wall forming the remaining side. The old brick barn comprised one flank of the square, arched openings displaying a winter's worth of stored hay and straw. This original brick building was augmented by a formidable concrete block structure from which issued the mooing of cows.

Across the square was a line of old brick rowhouses. The ones closest to the main house appeared inhabited, neat and tidy with painted shutters and potted plants on the stoop, while the dilapidated frontage of the ones at the far end nearer the outer wall were obviously uninhabitable and showed their extreme age. Three attached houses in the middle were currently under construction, with building supplies piled out front and a crew of workers bustling in and out.

But it was the main house that took her breath away. If you could even call it a house.

"What do you think?" Rocky asked, an obvious note of pride in his voice.

When he'd called it a farm, she'd imagined the hulking, dark brick buildings she'd seen from the train years ago. Not this. This was a castle. It wasn't that the building was so large, just two stories, but the gap-toothed crenelated roofline and delicate towers at either end made it feel like a story book castle.

An elegant, aging grand *signora*, the walls were mottled pink stucco. Where patches of stucco had flaked off, faded red brick showed through. Rows of tall windows lined both floors, each with a white stucco arch above and flanked by faded ochre shutters that glowed golden in the morning sun.

Bernadette was awestruck.

"It's a *castello*," Rocky said proudly. "Castello Maria."

"How old is it?" Bernadette asked.

"The main part of the house is four hundred years old."

"It's like something out of a fairy tale."

Rocky nodded. "A *castello* was a fortified farm. In medieval times fifteen families used to live and work here and for centuries it was its own little territory. My family struggled for many years to keep it going but in the last century it fell almost to ruin. My great-grandparents only lived in a small part of the main house and ran a small farm. In the past few years, the extended family have pulled together and turned it into an organic dairy – and an *agritourismo*, a farm B&B. They are turning the business around."

Taking her hand, he led her into a small courtyard at the side of the house where she was surprised to see that even now, in October, grapes hung in clusters from vines that clung to the delicate concrete arches of an upper loggia. It was easy to imagine Juliette herself stepping out on it to greet the morning.

She followed Rocky up a short flight of stairs and through a thick wooden door into a cloak room overflowing with rubber boots and jackets.

Rocky kicked off his shoes, calling, "Zia Sophia?"

A woman's voice answered back from deep inside the house, "*Si. Avanti.*"

Following his lead, Bernadette kicked off her boots and trailed Rocky down a hall and into a large kitchen. A tall woman wearing an apron stood facing them on the far side of a stainless-steel island, her back to the arch of an open brick hearth, hands on her hips and a frown on her face.

Rocky's whole demeanor had changed with his arrival at the farm. He walked over to his aunt with a boyish grin and kissed her soundly on both cheeks – a gesture she returned with grudging fondness and a spate of Italian.

Bernadette's Italian was barely basic, but she followed the conversation with the help of their gestures as Rocky introduced her to his aunt, who greeted her briskly and inquired whether they had eaten – *Hai mangiato?*

Suddenly, Bernadette realized she was starving. Rocky had rushed her out of the hotel restaurant an hour before, not giving her time to eat breakfast. Such as it was.

Sophia ushered them straight into the dining room, continuing to speak in Italian to Rocky, accompanying her words with exuberant hand gestures.

"The guests are still at breakfast, and we are welcome to join them," Rocky explained. He grinned. "She is horrified by how late they sleep. She wants to finish cleaning up the kitchen and get out to the creamery."

Sophia stopped and shook a finger at Rocky. He looked suitably chagrinned.

"She is angry that I have been here for five days and have only made it out to the farm once," he translated.

Bernadette was only listening with half her brain, the other half drinking in the details of the bright, beautiful dining room. Pastel arches framing distant vistas had been hand painted on the white plaster walls, and painted vines encircled each of the pillars that marched in a row down the center of the room. At the end, the sun streamed through three sets of glass doors onto two long rustic wooden tables, one on either side of the pillars. The tables provided seating for two dozen guests, but so far this morning only three guests were seated for breakfast.

On the wall opposite the doors, latticed windows looked out onto a kitchen garden. Below these windows, a table was spread with a tantalizing array of homecooked food. Bernadette's knees went weak as she took in the spread.

"They make all of this here at the *azienda*," Rocky said, handing Bernadette a plate. Taking one himself, he loaded it with prepared meats, freshly baked bread, cheeses, and a slice of a delectable apricot cake topped with a light dusting of icing sugar. In addition, two large bowls held mounds of mouth-watering pink and green grapes.

Bernadette quickly followed his lead and filled her plate, but managed to refrain from sampling the cake. Not with breakfast.

"What about the meat and cheese? Surely they don't make that."

"My uncle is a cheese maker, so, yes. They have a herd of cows – I'll show you later – and they make the cheese: ricotta, mozzarella, fontina. And everyone here makes sausage," he added with a very Italian one-shoulder shrug.

Once seated at the long table, they dug into their meal. Gradually guests trickled into the room. They all seemed to know each other and called greetings as they entered. A plump young woman in a white apron bustled in, chatting in Italian to the room in general while she filled their cups with steaming coffee and set a pitcher of cream on the table. Rocky stood to give her a hug, and she greeted him effusively. He introduced her to Bernadette as Valentina, another cousin. *Ciao* and more cheek kisses followed. At Valentina's urging, Bernadette gave in and went back for a piece of the apricot cake.

"Valentina said the B&B is full," Rocky said as Bernadette sat back down. "But then, this is one of the busiest weeks of the year. With all the activities going on in town, every accommodation is booked."

A man juggling a plate and glass of orange juice approached their table and indicated the empty seat next to Bernadette. He looked professorial in his tweed jacket, and asked in careful English, "May I join you?"

Chapter 13

Bernadette smiled at the man with the trim goatee. "Of course." She scooted over on the bench to make more room at the table.

"Are you here for the competitions?" he asked as he settled on the bench.

She nodded. "My partner and I are writing an article about Cremona for a travel magazine, and this seemed like the most exciting week to visit."

He smiled, his eyes sparkling behind his round, wire-framed glasses. "Indeed. Mondo Musica is always exciting. The entire world is here this week. I myself am from Munich. I am one of the Crown Competition judges." He took a mental step back, half stood in his seat and extended a hand to them each to shake. "Excuse my informality. My name is Helmut Roth."

Rocky and Bernadette both shook his hand and introduced themselves, then a rotund man in a green tweed suit carrying a plate piled with food sat down across from Roth.

"*Guten morgen*," he said to the group in general.

Helmut Roth replied in English. "Good morning, Gustaf. This is Mr. Falconi and Ms. Mallow, two reporters from America."

Canada, Bernadette mentally corrected.

Helmut continued. "This is my colleague, Gustaf Braun. He is from Munich also."

"Reporters," Gustaf exclaimed. "Are you here to report on the murder?"

"Murder?" Roth said, putting both hands on the table and leaning toward his friend. "What murder?"

"Have you not heard? The Scottish man was murdered in the Duomo Square last night. Amos Ballantyne. The man we met two days ago at Fanucci's shop. He is dead!" Gustaf seemed pleased to be the first to know.

Helmut's brow wrinkled above his glasses, which had slid down to perch on the end of his nose. "Dead? How did it happen?"

The other man shook his head. "I don't know. It is very mysterious. But from what I hear, it is almost certain he was murdered." As if to emphasise his point, he took a big bite of the pastry he held in his hand. Turning to Rocky, he asked, "Is that why you are here in Cremona?"

"No. We are writing a travel story about the city. How did you hear about the murder?"

Gustaf waved his cell phone. "Word is all over. Many people knew him. He had been around town all week, meeting people."

"Are you judging the competition too?" Bernadette asked.

Gustaf shook his head and took a gulp of coffee to wash down his latest mouthful of food. "I am a violin dealer. My business is in Munich. Did you know Mr. Ballantyne?"

"I did," Rocky said casually. "You met him?"

"Oh yes. I spoke to Ballantyne last week. He was curious about the process I use to authenticate violins. That is a big part of my business." Gustaf became serious. "People selling a violin want to get the best price, so they often come to me to get papers of authenticity. To say it was made by the person whose name is on the label inside. Less often I am asked by someone who has bought a violin to make sure it's worth what they paid." He shrugged. "Sometimes I can say yes, but sometimes I cannot."

"But you are more honest than some," Helmut put in.

Gustaf nodded as he cut into his large slice of apricot cake.

Bernadette frowned. "I don't understand. Why would someone want to change the label?"

Gustaf gave a half shrug. "If they are stolen, or forged."

"Forged?" Bernadette asked incredulously. "Violins?"

Helmut nodded gravely. "It happens. Nineteenth century German factories mass produced violins and regularly pasted Stradivarius labels inside them. Now, when someone finds one in the attic, they hope it is the real thing. That, however, any reputable dealer can spot." He waved a hand dismissively. "Everyone knows about those. I would not really call them 'forged'."

Gustaf added. "That is true. They are easy to see. The true forgeries are much harder to detect."

Rocky leaned forward. "How can you tell how old an instrument is?"

"It is not always easy, but I can usually tell just by look-ing," Gustaf said proudly. "However, there are some very good forgers in this city." He tipped his head knowingly. "There have been for hundreds of years."

"And Amos was asking about this?" Rocky asked.

"He was asking about certification, yes. And if any 'new' Stradivaris or other instruments by old masters had shown up on the market recently."

"Do new Strads still turn up?" Bernadette asked, slip-ping her hand into her bag for her note pad.

"With surprising frequency." Gustaf shook his head. "Of course, most of them are not what they claim to be. Most of these fakes never make it to my shop." He puffed out his chest. "It is well known that I cannot be bribed."

Bernadette's eyebrows went up. "Bribed?"

Helmut nodded. "Not everyone is as honest at Gustaf." The two men exchanged a telling look.

"Have any old instruments turned up recently?" Bernadette asked.

Gustaf nodded sagely. "Every year at Mondo Musica there are rumors. But who is to say if they are true."

Bernadette would have loved to pursue this intriguing topic, but an older man with a bushy beard, wearing jeans and a cardigan, standing outside the glass doors at the end of the dining room caught her eye. He motioned to Rocky, who nodded in return. Then the man turned and walked away.

"My uncle," Rocky said to Bernadette, setting his nap-kin on the table. "Are you finished?"

She downed the last of the delicious coffee Valentina had continued to refresh, and stood. Rocky reached across the table and shook hands with Helmut and Gustaf. "I'm sorry, but we must go. I hope we will meet again. Perhaps at the competition events? Or at Mondo Musica?"

"Or maybe here, again, at breakfast," Bernadette said hopefully, watching as Valentina began to clear the food from the table beneath the window.

Helmut nodded formally. "That would be my pleasure."

Bernadette followed Rocky to retrieve her boots and then out into the sunny courtyard where he greeted a man who was walking by, pushing a wheelbarrow full of bricks.

"Do you know everyone working here at the farm?" she asked.

"Pretty much. Most are family or neighbors. I lived here for ten months after I...left San Francisco."

Bernadette slid a side glance at him, but he was already forging ahead through the open wrought iron gate and out of the small courtyard, into the dusty plaza. He had never told her why he'd left the police force in San Francisco and although she was burning with curiosity, she knew he couldn't be pushed. She would just have to wait and hope that he would tell her in his own good time.

Chapter 14

Rocky's uncle was waiting by one of the arched openings to the old brick barn, a tortoiseshell cat rubbing figure eights around his ankles. His full grey beard hung down and brushed the brawny arms he'd crossed over his chest. He must have been in his sixties, but he was tall and strong across the shoulders, the result of arduous work on the farm.

As Rocky approached, his uncle unfolded his arms to give his nephew a heartfelt hug.

"Caio, Zio Ernesto," Rocky said, returning the embrace. Then he stepped back. "I'd like to introduce my partner, Bernadette Mallow."

Bernadette had noticed that Rocky became more formal when speaking to his family, even when he was speaking in English. She had a feeling that, in his head, he was translating from the more formal Italian.

She held out her hand. "*Piacere.*" It was one of the few Italian words she knew, but then, to cover her bases, she added in English, "So nice to meet you."

Ernesto gave her a quick once over as he took her hand. "*Piacere di conoscerla,*" he said. For a moment she was afraid he didn't speak English and was beginning to feel awkward about her lack of Italian, but then he said, "Come. I show you the car."

After the bright sunshine of the yard, the interior of the barn felt cool and dark. Big round hay bales, piled to the rafters, sweetly scented the air. Decorative openings high in the brickwork allowed shafts of light to fall into the back of the barn onto a small, tarped mound. Ernesto tugged off the cover to expose a tiny, baby-blue vehicle that looked more like a Pixar car than an actual mode of transportation.

"Classic," Rocky said with satisfaction, a big grin on his face.

Bernadette looked at him in surprise, but Ernesto nodded in agreement. "*Sì. Un Cinquecento.*"

"What year?" Rocky asked.

"Nineteen seventy," Ernesto said with obvious pride.

The tiny car was wedged between stacked hay bales, front and back, and Bernadette didn't see how they would get it out, short of moving the pile of six-foot diameter bales.

Two men dressed in denim overalls sauntered into the barn. A spate of Italian flew back and forth along with back slapping and surprising kisses of Bernadette's cheeks.

"My cousins," Rocky explained briefly. "Charlie and Leonardo."

More cousins? How many cousins did he have?

Then, without further discussion, the four men positioned themselves each at one corner of the car and, on Ernesto's grunted command, lifted the tiny car with ease and set it down in the open space of the barn. Dust motes spangled the sunshine. Bernadette sneezed.

"*Buona fortuna*," Charlie and Leonardo said in unison.

"*Grazie*," she said, hoping it was the correct response.

Rocky was examining the car carefully. The top half was painted baby blue. Rust crept up the white fenders and around the spotted chrome trim. The roof was a good six inches below Bernadette's chin and, peeking in the open roof hatch, she saw that the black seats were in fair condition, only split in a few places along the seams. The painted metal dashboard was simple with one big round dial in front of the driver.

"I hope it will start," Rocky said to his uncle.

"*Si*. We had it on the road last year, and I recharged the battery yesterday. She just needs some *benzina*."

Ernesto disappeared and returned moments later with a rusty red gas can. He lifted the Fiat emblem on the front hood and poured the gas into the pipe hidden behind it. Then he tossed a key to Rocky who caught it in mid-air.

Rocky climbed eagerly into the driver's seat, fooled with the levers on the floor between the seats, put the key in the ignition and turned it. The motor grudgingly groaned, turned over – then sputtered to a stop.

Ernesto muttered to himself as he rounded to the back of the car. The trunk hood creaked open exposing a diminutive motor inside. He squirted something into the engine – Bernadette had no idea what – and gave Rocky the signal to try it again.

Rocky reached between the seats, lifted a lever, turned the key, then grinned as the engine turned over and ran. It was loud and rough, but it didn't quit. Ernesto slammed the engine compartment closed, pulled a rag out of his pocket and wiped his hands with satisfaction.

"Hop in," Rocky called to Bernadette over the clatter of the motor.

The passenger door creaked loudly as she wrenched it open and climbed inside. It was a tight fit, but kind of fun. Rocky put the car in gear, and they chugged out of the barn.

His uncle and cousins followed and, as Rocky yelled his thanks over the noise of the engine, Ernesto hollered back, "Dinner. Saturday night."

Rocky gave him a thumbs up, and the Fiat chugged away around the courtyard. As they passed the house, Sophia emerged from the main front door. Wiping her hands on her apron, she called out to Rocky. He slowed to listen, and to Bernadette's surprise, his good humor evaporated. He nodded a curt reply and as the car lurched on around the plaza, he gave only cursory wave to the construction crew at the rowhouses who hooted and waved in reply.

A big iron gate hung from one hinge off the end of the crumbling brick wall. The Fiat coughed, then lurched through the gate and onto a narrow dirt road. When they reached the main road, Rocky took the corner and headed back toward Cremona. Bernadette was glad to see that the car ran more smoothly as he geared up, but it was hard to tell if the rattle and bounce beneath them was caused by the potholes in the road or the car itself.

As Rocky shifted gears again, Bernadette glanced down and saw asphalt flying beneath his feet.

She gasped. "There's no floor!"

He glanced at her feet. "You have a floor. I'll be fine. This car is just what we need in the city. Easy to park. You'll see."

Bernadette gripped the handle on the dashboard, hoping the car wouldn't fly apart before they got to town. The noise reverberating up through the hole in the floor made conversation difficult, but Bernadette suspected Rocky's mind was on whatever had been Zia Sophia's final message. It had obviously dampened his mood.

When they reached the edge of Cremona, Rocky parked the car in front of a café housed on the ground floor of one of the modern, low-rise apartment buildings that lined the road on the outskirts of town.

"I don't need any more coffee," Bernadette said.

Rocky stared straight ahead, hands on the wheel. "No, but we should talk."

She glanced at him briefly. She did want to know what was going on, and since it was impossible to have a serious conversation over the road noise in the Fiat, she got out of the car and followed him into the café.

The décor on the inside of the café was as modern and sterile as the outside. She ordered another cappuccino and Rocky ordered a double espresso. Although the room was almost empty, Rocky steered them outside to a black iron table. Not the most scenic spot on the side of the busy roadway surrounded by low-rise apartments, but they were alone on the small patio.

"What's up?" Bernadette asked brightly, hoping to lighten the mood.

Rocky's jaw was firm, she would almost say clenched. "My cousin Niccolo wants to see me. That was the message from Sophia."

"What does he want?"

"He wants me to identify the body."

"What do you mean he wants you to identify the body?" A shrill note had crept into her voice, and she quickly looked around, glad to see they were still alone.

She lowered her voice. "Is Niccolo with the police?"

"Didn't I tell you? He's an *Ispettore*. An Inspector. He must have discovered my connection to Hamish."

"How could he have found that out so soon?"

Rocky shrugged. "It wouldn't take much. Just ask around at the hotel bar. I'm sure people saw us talking last night."

"Okay. So you go and tell them what you know about Amos, I mean Hamish. That should be it."

Rocky didn't answer, just watched the cars whizzing by.

Bernadette's eyes narrowed. "Shouldn't it? Do you know what got him..." She swallowed. "Killed?"

"Of course not." Rocky knocked back the double shot and slapped the cup on the metal table. "I have no idea why he was killed, but I know him – knew him – pretty well, so I can at least identify the body. He doesn't have much family, just a sister in Scotland. Inverness, I think. But yes, I can identify the body. And tell them his real name."

Rocky stared silently into his empty cup. Finally he said, almost to himself, "I know. I should let it go. But we go way back. I owe it to Hamish to make sure the cops find his murderer." He stared at the road, then drank the last trickle of coffee from the tiny cup. "You done? Let's go."

She wasn't done, but she hadn't wanted the drink in the first place, so she nodded and stood up.

"I'll drop you at the hotel," he said as they got into the Fiat. "You don't have to come to the station."

Bernadette buckled herself in. "I'm coming with you."

She was quite sure there was more to the Rocky-and-Hamish story than he was letting on, and she was determined to find out what it was.

Chapter 15

The police station stood on a main street in the old city, one of the spokes of the wheel that met at the Duomo square. Wider than most streets in the historic district with two lanes for cars and a line painted down the middle, Rocky was able to squeeze the tiny Cinquecento into an empty angled parking space in front of the building.

"I told you this car would be perfect," he said.

As with all the streets in the old town, the buildings pushed right up to a narrow sidewalk. For an official building, the pale-yellow façade of the police station was relatively plain. The ground floor windows were masked with ornate ironwork and above each window a crest was molded into the stucco. A massive wooden door shuttered a high arch, wide enough to drive a carriage through and directly over the door, a narrow iron balcony held an Italian flag and one sporting the Cremonese crest. A small unobtrusive sign on the wall beside the door read, *Questura*.

Rocky opened a regular-sized door in the archway and they walked through into a short corridor that led to a generous courtyard, a hidden town square in the center of the block, complete with trees and a few scattered benches. The buildings that surrounded the square were peppered with doors, but Rocky seemed to know where he was going and led Bernadette through a door immediately to their left.

Inside, a uniformed police officer stood behind a counter in front of a glass window that separated the foyer from the squad room. The glass sound-proofed the foyer, but Bernadette could see that the room was a hive of activity.

"Ispettore Falconi?" Rocky asked.

The officer at the desk turned and looked through the window.

Following his gaze, Bernadette spotted Niccolo, the tallest officer in the crowded room. He was talking – or rather listening – to a shorter, powerfully built man in a dark suit who she recognized as one of the men from the restaurant the previous evening, the one who had stopped at Hamish's table on his way out. A small circle of officers had gathered around them and he was pointing at Niccolo's chest with his index finger.

Niccolo looked up and when he saw Rocky and Bernadette, a look of recognition, or possibly relief, flashed across his face. He broke into the diatribe and the other man flashed a look in their direction. Then, with a flick of his hand, he indicated Niccolo should go, following him through the door to the reception area.

Niccolo greeted them with, "*Ciao, grazie,*" then waited for the other man to join them before making formal introductions. He introduced Rocky in Italian, then switched to English to introduce Bernadette. "And this is his partner, Bernadette Mallow, a travel writer. They are working on a piece on Cremona for *Let's Travel* magazine. I wish to introduce Comissario Grassi."

The Commissioner nodded briskly to them both, then turned to Rocky. "Ispettore Falconi tells me you knew the victim."

Rocky nodded, and said carefully, "We had met, years ago. I was surprised to see him in the bar last night."

Grassi's eyes narrowed as he appeared to think this over. Then he dismissed them with a wave of his hand. "Ispettore Falconi will take you to see the body. We hope you can identify him. We would like to wrap this case up quickly. I hope you understand that this is not a usual occurrence in our town and that you can see fit to omit it from your article."

Rocky nodded. "I understand. Not good for business."

The Commissioner hesitated. For a moment it looked like he had more to say, but then changed his mind. In the end he just nodded once and returned to the busy squad room.

When the door closed behind him, Niccolo spoke to Rocky in rapid-fire Italian.

"No problem," Rocky responded, steering the conversation back into English.

Niccolo turned to Bernadette and nodded. "Hello, Bernadette."

"Hello," she said, surprised by his formal manner and beginning to wonder if she should have gone back to the hotel after all. But she felt she owed Rocky and wanted to support him. He stood by her when she was implicated in the murder in Mexico so the least she could do was stick by him now that his friend had been murdered.

"I am glad you agreed to come," Niccolo said to Rocky. "Comissario Grassi is in a hurry to solve this crime and he is breathing down my neck. It is bad for the whole community to have foreigners murdered on our streets, particularly during Mondo Musica."

He led the way down a corridor, out a glass door and along a paved walk and into building across the square.

"You can wait here," Niccolo said to Bernadette, indicating a row of wooden benches that lined the long corridor. "There is no reason for you to put yourself through this."

The grim vibrations that emanated through the double metal doors under the sign *Obitorio* convinced Bernadette that Niccolo was right. This was enough support. She didn't need to see the body.

As Rocky followed his cousin through the swinging doors, Bernadette sank gratefully onto a bench, wondering what kind of tragedy in the past would warrant seating for so many in the waiting area of the morgue.

* * *

One thing Rocky had discovered years ago – the smell of disinfectant never really disguised the reek of death. Now, as always, the combination of the two overwhelmed him, turning his stomach. Viewing dead bodies never got easy and in his years as a cop he'd seen many, often in worse shape than this. But this one was personal. Hamish was a friend. At the sight of the lifeless face, it hit him – he'd never hear that obnoxious, contagious laugh again. Never get dragged into one of Hamish's poorly thought-out schemes. Never again have a night cap to-gether at a hole-in-the-wall bar.

His friend hadn't been satisfied with the story in front of him – had always been looking for the story behind the story. In their younger, more reckless days when they were covering war zones, Hamish always looked out for the little guy, covering the plight of civilians who through no fault of their own were suffering. Although they'd both mellowed and were doing what could be called puff pieces by comparison, Rocky was sure Hamish was following a story behind a story here in Cremona. He was equally sure that this something was important enough to get him killed.

He spoke to Niccolo in Italian. "His name is Hamish Gladstone."

Niccolo didn't look surprised. "That is the name I see here. But what we want to know is why was the name on the hotel records and his passport Amos Ballantyne?"

Rocky sighed. He wasn't surprised that in this day of facial recognition software it had taken less than a day before the police discovered Hamish's real name. "He was a reporter, undercover as Amos Ballantyne. He'd been published in the London Observer, among other papers and magazines."

"What was he doing here?"

Rocky shook his head. "I don't know. I hadn't seen him in years and didn't know he was here until last night when we met accidentally in the hotel bar. We only spoke for a few minutes. Since we were in public, he didn't talk about why he was here, and I didn't ask." Rocky looked down at the body on the slab. "I thought there would be time."

"How long have you known him?" Niccolo asked, making notes on his clipboard.

Rocky took a deep breath, trying to steady himself as their colorful history flickered through his mind. "Six years, I guess. We met in Aleppo, Syria. It was my first job as a photojournalist, right after I lived here."

Niccolo nodded. "I remember. Does he have any family?"

Rocky stared down on the lifeless form on the slab. "A sister. Lives in Inverness."

Niccolo thanked the attendant, and Rocky watched the man soberly cover his old friend's face one last time.

"What was the cause of death?" Rocky asked.

"Gunshot to the heart. Looked like a robbery. What do you Americans call it? A mugging? They took his wallet and watch. The Comissario saw him right before his death and noticed the watch. Very expensive."

Rocky nodded. He'd noticed it too, part of the rich collector disguise. "Isn't a gunshot unusual for a mugging?"

"Mugging gone wrong, perhaps."

"Sounds more like a premeditated hit to me," Rocky said.

"Maybe," Niccolo allowed. "But why?"

Rocky shook his head. He didn't know, but he was determined to find out why someone wanted his old friend dead.

Chapter 16

Bernadette sat on the hard wooden bench outside the morgue, tapping her toes on the tile floor, the sound echoing hollowly down the long hall. A breeze brushed her cheeks, and she glanced at the doors at each end of the hall, but both were firmly closed. She sighed. Probably not the wind, then. More likely the stirring of spirits of people who had passed through these halls. She'd never been in a morgue before but wasn't surprised by the feeling. She often felt whispers of the dead in cemeteries and places that had witnessed violent death.

Suddenly the door beside her flew open. She jumped to her feet as Rocky and his cousin came out of the morgue. She didn't known how she expected him to react to seeing his friend's body – with sadness, or possibly anger, but not with the hard look of determination she now saw on his face.

"Do you have time for coffee?" Rocky asked Niccolo.

Niccolo looked at his phone. "It's time for lunch. Let's grab some *tramezzini.* There's a lunch bar down the street."

The fresh air on Bernadette's cheeks brushed the ghoulish thoughts away and as they walked the long block to the café, she inhaled deeply, clearing her nose of the lingering smell of disinfectant and death.

Inside the crowded lunch bar, they lined up to order coffee and sandwiches piled with salami and roasted vegetables, grilled flat in a panini press until golden brown. When a window table became available, people waiting glanced at their group – recognizing Niccolo, she suspected – and indicated that they should take the table. Cremona might be considered a city, but the old *centro* seemed more like a village.

When they settled at the table, Rocky uncharacteristically ignored his sandwich and peppered his cousin with questions. "Any other suspicious injuries?" he asked in a low voice.

"He has a bruise on his head, as if he fell on the stone," Niccolo said, his mouth full of salami sandwich. "The *medico* thought he may have fallen against the wall. And one bullet hole in the chest."

Rocky took a bite of his sandwich and chewed thoughtfully. "I don't think it was a robbery."

Niccolo stopped eating. "Why do you say that?"

"He was always sticking his nose where it wasn't wanted. You should look at his record."

Niccolo cocked his head. "Prison?"

"No. Work record. He brought a number of frauds to light, all over the globe, and some big tycoons to their knees. He must have had enemies, but we haven't been close in years so I don't know what he was doing here."

"Covering the convention?" Niccolo suggested.

Rocky snorted. "He hadn't gone that soft. And why would he use an alias for that? No, he had to be digging into something bigger. Something illegal. Last night in the bar he indicated he was onto something big, but there was no chance to find out more. What do you know about what he'd been doing since he got to town?"

"I know he interviewed one of the local dealers, Alessandro Fanucci, and a local violin maker, Marco Passero." Niccolo shrugged. "Maybe other people too, I don't know yet. Although those are two highly respected men, I have long thought Fanucci must have something going on the side." He took another bite of his sandwich and shook his head. "But I can't believe either of them would resort to murder."

"Passero," Rocky said thoughtfully.

"You know him?"

He shook his head. "Met him briefly this morning. Mia apprentices with him."

"That's right. I'm going to speak to them both this afternoon." Niccolo wiped his lips with his napkin and stood, tossing it on the table. "You." He pointed at Rocky. "Keep out of it."

As his cousin walked away, Rocky picked up his sandwich and took a bite.

"What made him say that?" Bernadette asked.

Rocky took his time to finish chewing, watching out the window as Niccolo walked down the street, back to the Questura. "I helped him with a case last time I was here."

"Really," Bernadette said thoughtfully. "Niccolo's boss didn't seem to know you."

Rocky shook his head. "It was before his time."

"The Commissioner was in the restaurant last night," Bernadette said. "He stopped at Hamish's table."

"I noticed that too," Rocky agreed.

"Well, that's a good thing, don't you think? I mean, surely he will take this case seriously since he actually knew the victim."

Rocky's eyes narrowed.

"Hamish," Bernadette quickly amended.

Rocky didn't reply, just attacked his sandwich again.

Finally, Bernadette put down her sandwich and sighed. "You're not going to keep out of it, are you?"

"I was going to, but seeing Hamish laid out like that..." Something hardened in Rocky's expression.

She regarded him seriously, her sandwich forgotten, then nodded. "For now, though, we have our own work to do. We have time to go to the museum before the opening of Mondo Musica tonight. The police are moving on the case. I don't think there's anything we can do right now."

"Maybe not right now," Rocky said. "But I owe it to Hamish to do what I can to help find his killer."

Chapter 17

T hat evening, as the Fiat sped toward the *Fiera* on the outskirts of town, Bernadette looked out the window at the gathering gloom.

"The museum was well done," she said. "All of the instruments were beautiful and it was interesting to see Stradivari's tools. I hadn't realized there were so many other important makers in the seventeenth century whose violins are still in use today. I'd love to hold one."

"You might have to be satisfied with seeing them behind glass," Rocky said. "But we may get lucky."

When they reached the modern arena on the outskirts of town, Rocky squeezed the tiny car into a minute space at the end of a row of scooters. In the dusky evening glow, spotlights illuminated a row of flags of a dozen nations fluttering in the breeze. Bernadette felt a sudden thrill at being part of this international event, the United Nations of the violin world.

Falling into the line of people waiting to get in, Bernadette watched as more cars pulled up to the drop off zone and glittering guests stepped out. Many of the women wore fancy cocktail dresses with shiny evening jackets. Cremona may be an ancient city, but they were only sixty miles from the fashion capital of Milan, and the people of Cremona wanted the world to know it.

Rocky looked good, as usual. His Armani jacket – she'd checked the label the previous day when it was hung on the back of a chair – seemed to work for any occasion. Bernadette looked down at her little black travel dress and plain knit jacket, wishing she'd brought some sparkly jewelry to liven it up. But they were only journalists, not guests of honor, so it would have to do.

There was a crush at the door, but Rocky flashed a brilliant smile and waved the participant passes Mia had given them at the female attendant and before Bernadette knew it, he had taken her arm and guided her into the immense hall.

Hundreds of booths with either red or black walls lined the red carpeted aisles, ready for the show. Makers and dealers milled around in the vicinity of their allotted spaces, but many had left young people, apprentices Bernadette supposed, to guard their stock. An invitation-only event, there was little chance of theft, and noticing that most of the key players went directly to the broad, open staircase to the restaurant upstairs, she and Rocky headed there as well. By the time the speeches began a few minutes later, they had found the bar and had drinks in their hands.

And there were speeches galore, all in Italian. Bernadette's attention wandered away from the podium at the front of the restaurant to search out the attendees she recognized scattered through the audience.

In the crowd, she recognized many of the people she had seen at the hotel the night before, including the Cremona Crown competitors and their handlers. She saw Rocky's cousin Mia and her boss Maestro Passero, although they were not standing together. Across the crowded room, she spotted Comissario Grassi, Niccolo's boss, in black evening dress, standing next to a sparkly, middle-aged woman whom Bernadette guessed must be his wife. A few feet away from him was the rotund mustachioed dealer – Alessandro Fanucci, Hamish had called him. He was with a woman, too, but she was half his age, six inches taller than he was and stunningly beautiful. He turned and spoke to a tall, solid man next to him whom Bernadette hadn't seen before.

She glanced at Rocky and saw he too was checking out the crowd. He had his camera out and was photographing the honorees, then swung it casually across the room to where this group of men were standing, snapping candid shots as he did.

Niccolo suddenly appeared beside them. Rocky asked in a low voice, "Who is the big guy with Fanucci?"

Niccolo gave the men a quick glance, then turned his eyes back to the stage. He leaned toward Rocky and said something so quietly that Bernadette didn't catch anything except the name, "Massimo Cassiglio."

A wave of applause broke out and Bernadette automatically joined in.

"Speeches are almost over," Niccolo said to them both. "Want to come to the after-party at Fanucci's?"

Bernadette's eyes widened. She nodded. Passero and Grassi would probably be there and, other than herself and

Rocky, they were the last known people to see Hamish alive.

Chapter 18

Fanucci's villa was on a rise outside the town. Unlike the gates at the Falconi family farm that hung permanently askew, Fanucci's ornate iron gates swung open and closed silently behind them on well-oiled hinges. Once inside, the white gravel driveway glowed ghostly in the moonlight, rows of well-spaced Lombardy poplar trees guarding the route like sentries.

"Niccolo said the name of the guy with Fanucci at the event tonight was Cassiglio, and he is probably in the mob," Rocky said. "He's got a finger in all kinds of things here in town. Whitewashes his dirtier dealings with charity contributions. Apparently he donates to the Policeman's charities, too."

"Smart," Bernadette said.

"Puts Niccolo's boss in a sticky position," Rocky said grimly.

"I'm glad to see Nicco's on duty tonight."

"He's been assigned to Hamish's case. The police commissioner seems eager to get this case closed."

They broke out of the trees and got their first view of the villa's well-lit white façade, bright against the dark sky. The roof of the villa was a complex design, with an imposing peak held high by soaring fluted pillars over the front entrance.

The drive circled a glowing statue of entwined lovers and Bernadette stuck her head out the open skylight and said in an awestruck voice, "Oh my God. Are those *statues* on the roof?"

Rocky ducked his head to peer up through the Fiat's front window. "Yup."

"It's a friggin' castle!"

Rocky grinned. "I seem to remember you said that about the farm, too. But this time I would have to agree. It is pretty impressive."

"Who knew the violin business was so lucrative?" Bernadette said.

Rocky nodded. "Fanucci is making a killing on something."

Fingers of fog from a stream at the edge of the garden crept across the well-kept lawn. Cars were lined up on the driveway and in front of the villa. Rocky found a tiny space and parked their baby-blue Cinquecento on the edge of the group. It looked very modest in the line-up of luxury cars. Except, Rocky noticed, for one at the far end – an old, green, Lada station wagon.

A group of men were smoking at one corner of the house and watched as Rocky and Bernadette made their way to the entrance.

"Those must be the drivers," Rocky said.

"Maybe you should join them," Bernadette suggested.

"I might learn as much from them as we do inside. But not tonight." He took her arm as they walked past the parked Ferraris, Maseratis, and – Rocky circled a car to find the insignia – even a Bugatti Chiron.

The second story windows were dark and shuttered, but the ground floor was ablaze with light. In the opulent front foyer, small groups of people stood chatting, drinks in hand. Rocky didn't recognize anyone so they continued down two broad marble steps into a large, high-ceilinged reception room packed with people where the noise level rose considerably. Making their way to a crowded bar, they ordered drinks, then retired to a quiet corner to review the scene.

Most of the guests seemed to be Italian, or at least were speaking Italian. Hands flew in gesture and laughter rang out, echoing off the high, ornately carved plaster ceiling. The contestants from the Cremona Crown and their handlers were here, scattered about the room, as were Gustaf Braun and Helmut Roth, with whom they had breakfasted at the farm. Comissario Grassi and his wife arrived, her blue sequined dress hanging on her emaciated body, a sharp contrast to Massimo Cassiglio's girlfriend who entered right behind her, a shiny black dress plastered to her lush figure.

Rocky spotted Cassiglio in the foyer, speaking quietly to two men. Although dressed in black, they were casually dressed and Rocky deduced they were not party guests. They hung on Cassiglio's every word, then one of them gave a quick one-finger salute and they both hurried out the door. Cassiglio shot his cuffs as if to say, "job done," then caught up with his party in the main salon where they joined Fanucci at the bar.

A moment later, Niccolo arrived. He made eye contact with Rocky and Bernadette from the doorway and headed across the room toward them. Rocky glanced at Fanucci. He had seen the police officer arrive and an angry cloud blackened the portly man's face. He motioned to the commissioner who was at the bar, waving a hand toward Niccolo who was now standing next to Rocky and Bernadette.

Rocky watched with interest as the police commissioner nodded to Fanucci and hurried straight to them. Commissioner Grassi moved through the crowd like a battleship carving a path through water, the guests parting as he passed and reassembling in a flurried little wake of speculation behind him.

The commissioner kept his tone low, but his eyes narrowed. "What are you doing here?"

"Following up on some leads," Niccolo said calmly. "You may remember that Hamish Gladstone was looking to purchase an expensive violin, and all the key players he spoke to are here tonight."

Exactly, Rocky thought.

The commissioner switched to Italian. "You are embarrassing our host. I must ask you to leave and to do your investigating at a more appropriate time."

Niccolo's face remained calm – but Rocky saw a muscle twitch in his cheek.

"And please take your friends with you," Grassi added in English, looking at Rocky and Bernadette. "I'm sorry, but this is a private party."

Rocky glanced at Niccolo. He had to admit, in his nondescript clothes, the universal police detective's uniform that fairly screamed "cop," his cousin looked even more out of place than he and Bernadette did.

Bernadette stepped in. "We are sorry, Comissario. Please excuse us, we didn't realize."

He accepted her apology with a nod and turned away.

Bernadette moved toward the door, and the others followed wordlessly.

Once they were outside, though, Niccolo thumped the meaty side of his fist against one of the stone pillars. "*Che cavolo!* He is not doing his job. I swear he is a limp rag when it comes to Fanucci, but I cannot ignore a direct order."

Bernadette stifled a yawn. "I don't think we are going to find out anything more tonight anyway. It's been a long day and I'm still jet lagged. Let's go."

Rocky agreed, but as he climbed into the Fiat, he and Nicco exchanged a hard look. This wasn't over. Not by a long shot.

Thursday, Day Three

Chapter 19

The following morning was the first round of the Cremona Crown Competition. Bernadette enjoyed classical music, even if she did not go to many concerts, and considered this a rare opportunity to hear these excellent young musicians. Each contestant played their choice of one of Bach's Partitas, Numbers 1, 2 or 3, and as the tenth contestant took the stage, she shifted in her seat. They were all excellent players, but after three hours of sitting on the hard, folding chairs in the makeshift auditorium, she was having a tough time focussing.

She glanced at Rocky, who had his arms crossed and eyes closed. She would have enjoyed this more if he hadn't been so agitated. When he was upset, the man gave off waves of energy, vibrations that would have rattled her nervous system from across the room and were particularly distracting when they were sitting shoulder to shoulder. Rocky thought he hid his feelings behind that cool mask he wore, but Bernadette could read him like a book. He was upset about his friend's murder – who wouldn't be? – and couldn't rest until the murderer was caught. As usual, he didn't want to get involved, but with his background as a San Francisco police detective, she imagined the apparent lack of movement by the Italian police was driving him crazy.

The fizz she had felt emanating from him when they first arrived at the concert hall had lessened though, and now he seemed to be dozing. Bernadette shifted on the hard seat and turned her attention back to the stage. She tried her best to make notes about the contestants, to differentiate how they played, but despite all the years of violin lessons she'd taken as a child she felt hopelessly out of her depths.

Right now Zahid, the Middle Eastern contestant, was playing. His tone was noticeably different, sharper, confident, but somehow more discordant to her ear than the others. He managed to make the classical European piece sound faintly exotic.

The five judges seated on a raised dais in the second row looked like the adjudicators on her favorite reality TV show. She recognized Helmut Roth from breakfast at the farm, but she didn't know the other four. Checking her program, she saw there were also two Italians, one Swiss and one American from New York. All had long lists of credentials, but nothing jumped out at her as story-worthy. She would make an appointment to speak to Helmut again before the contest was over.

The repetition of the program allowed her mind to wander and she wondered if it was necessary for her and Rocky to attend all of the preliminary rounds. This one was nearly over and according to the contest rules, at the end of this session half of the contestants would be eliminated. That would leave seven for the next round where, she saw with dismay, they would all be playing the same piece, a modern concerto composed specially for the festival by an Italian composer she had never heard of. She was interested to hear it. Once. Not seven times. She wondered if they could take a pass on that one.

The final performance was scheduled for Sunday afternoon in the Opera Hall with the top four finalists each playing a concerto by a major classical composer of their choice, backed by a full orchestra. Rocky had already mentioned that he wanted to be there to take photographs, and of course she wanted to be there too.

Zahid bowed and left the stage to polite applause. All of the contestants were so accomplished that she wondered how the judges could find fault with any of their performances.

Bernadette glanced at Rocky. He was still sitting with his eyes closed, camera slung around his neck. She could have sworn he was asleep, but he'd fooled her before.

Studying her program, she saw there were only two contestants to go: Jay, the American, and Tatiana, the Romanian girl.

Jay took the stage next. *Took command of the stage*, she wrote in her notes. He walked to the center, stopped, then slowly surveyed the audience. He gave a nod to the judges, then raised his instrument to his shoulder, closed his eyes and began to play. The music poured from his violin filling every corner of the auditorium with glorious sound; rich vibrations Bernadette felt to her core.

Rocky's eyes sprang open, and he glanced at Bernadette, then rose smoothly to his feet. This wasn't the first time she'd noticed his ability to go from sound asleep to fully functioning in seconds. He had chosen a side-aisle seat again, as always positioning himself in advance for accessibility to the best shots.

Jay kept his eyes closed as he played, frowning slightly, swaying gently as the music flowed effortlessly from his instrument. The bow bounced lightly in a bubbly passage, his hair falling appealingly over his forehead. He was the whole package: flawless musician, consummate performer and as good looking as a movie star. In Bernadette's opinion, he was the best contestant so far.

He finished with a race up to what she was sure was the violin's highest note, then dropped to finish on a strongly bowed string. It was a powerful ending. His eyes stayed closed for the time it took for the note to reverberate, then fade in the hall. Was he really entranced, Bernadette wondered, or did he keep his eyes closed for effect? Either way, he looked like the music still held him in its sway as it still held the crowd. Then he opened his eyes and looked at the audience and everyone, Bernadette included, burst into thundering applause.

Jay took in the room with a faint, smug smile, bowed deeply and left the stage. Job done.

Rocky had been silently taking pictures of the young man right up to his final bow, then he sat back down beside Bernadette and folded his arms across his chest again. This time, however, he stayed awake and alert.

Bernadette's pulse quickened. Although she knew who the final contestant was, she glanced at her program, then at Rocky. "Tatiana," she mouthed. He nodded.

An expectant hush fell over the room. Tatiana walked out onto center stage, raised her violin to her shoulder and waited. The room held its breath.

Her dress was plain compared to the other contestants, a shapeless black sheath, tied clumsily at the waist, and although she clearly didn't have the financial backing of most of the other contestants, she stood proudly, chin raised. Bernadette supposed that ideally, in a socialist country like Romania, children with talent, regardless of their social standing, would have a shot at the training they needed to reach the heights Tatiana had achieved.

Then she raised her bow and started to play. Music rolled through the auditorium like a wave. Bernadette sat in stunned silence. Although she had already heard the same melody many times that afternoon, under Tatiana's bow it was magical. Bernadette closed her eyes as the melody wound around her like a snake, hypnotic and seductive. She was at a loss to explain whether the source of the enchantment was the violin or the player, but however it happened, she was transported to a land of dreams.

She was aware, however, that Rocky was on the job, camera raised. When the piece was finished, Tatiana put her hands at her sides, the violin and bow behind her back, chin thrust forward, and bowed from the waist to eager applause. Then, without a smile, almost like an automaton, she walked off the stage.

Bernadette looked at Rocky. He was still standing, but now his camera was aimed at Tatiana's coach, who was on her feet and clapping wildly.

When the applause subsided, Helmut Roth tapped on a microphone, drawing the audience's attention to the raised dais where the judges sat. He cleared his throat and spoke. "There will be a short break while the judges confer, and then we will announce the contestants who will move on to the next round." He followed as the line of judges exited through a door, stage right.

"Looks like Jay might have some competition," Bernadette said.

Rocky put his camera bag over his shoulder. "Looks like. Let's see if these passes can get us backstage."

Chapter 20

B ernadette stood and stretched, happy to stand after
sitting for so long, and followed Rocky into the contestant's green room behind the stage. Energy bounced off
the walls of the packed room as contestants beamed nerves
and excitement while their parents and teachers hovered
over them as if they were coiffured pets at a dog show.

As usual Rocky took off, following his own agenda and
leaving Bernadette to look for someone to interview. This
was, after all, the main story they had been sent to cover.
The trick would be to figure out in advance who the top
two or three contestants were going to be and follow them
through the competition. So far, she would choose Jay and
Tatiana to be in the final flight. And Una, the Korean girl,
and Angelo, whose photograph Rocky was taking at that
moment in a well-lit corner across the room. As the Italian
entry, Angelo certainly showed the national bravado that
added to his performance. And, as the host entry, the hint
of a crown prince in waiting. But besides Rocky, he was
surrounded by Italian journalists, so Bernadette turned
her attention elsewhere, looking for an easier quarry to
pick out of the herd.

Tatiana stood quietly by herself in another corner, her violin tucked under her arm. Bernadette pulled her phone out of her purse as she approached and turned on the voice recording app. Although Tatiana returned her smile, Bernadette felt it wasn't entirely genuine. There was something sad, almost haunted, in the girl's eyes. And she *was* a girl, looked barely a teenager, although Bernadette couldn't help wondering if it was the oversized dress that made her look like a child playing dress up.

She reminded Bernadette of Degas' delicate sculpture of the young ballet dancer, an awkward girl made of beeswax with a real ribbon tying back her sculpted hair, a detail that made her seem all the more fragile. Although copied many times, the original ground-breaking sculpture wore a limp tutu of real cotton and silk, and linen slippers. Calling this one *Little Dancer aged Fourteen*, Degas managed to catch both vulnerability and pride in her stance. Maybe that was why Tatiana reminded Bernadette of the statue. She held her head high, chin thrust out, like Degas' ballet dancer.

Bernadette blinked to clear the image. "Tatiana, I wanted to tell you how much I loved your performance. I was transported."

"Thank you,'" she said, but her eyes narrowed thoughtfully, causing Bernadette to wonder how much English the girl understood.

"How long have you been playing?"

"All my life."

That answered that question. Although her accent was heavy, her English came easily. Bernadette smiled. "How old are you?"

"Seventeen."

"Wow. You are amazingly good."

This brought the first hint of a smile to Tatiana's lips, but her expression quickly shut down when her coach Mirela swooped in on their conversation.

"Yes, Tatiana is the best player here. I am sure she is possible to win the first prize." Her accent was strong, but her English was good as well. Her predator's smile showed a row of white teeth against her dusky complexion. Her shiny black hair was swept back in a stylish chignon on the back of her head. As usual, her clothes were ostentatious. A tight black knit dress with a deep sequined neckline showed under her signature hot pink coat. "I am Mirela Florescu, Tatiana's coach and travel companion."

After shaking Mirela's hand, Bernadette turned back to Tatiana. "Where in Romania do you live?"

"I now live in Bucharest."

"Tatiana is the youngest student ever admitted to our National University of Music," Mirela said proudly. "Quite an honor."

"I'm sure it is." Bernadette turned her recorder back toward Tatiana. "That is a lovely violin you have."

The girl brought the instrument out from behind her back so that Bernadette could study it. "It is not mine. It is on loan for the year from the university collection."

"It is a Bergonzi," Mirela added quickly. "Almost three hundred years old. It has an amazing sound."

Bernadette nodded in agreement, but smiled at Tatiana and said, "Surely most of the credit must go to Tatiana."

Heat slid down Bernadette's back like a warm hand as Rocky came up behind her. She told herself her reaction was only because he was her partner, but she knew it was actually something more. Something that started six months ago in Mexico.

He was all charming smiles for Mirela who, with his arrival, turned from Cruella De Vil to a fawning diva in two seconds flat. Bernadette rolled her eyes. How did he do it? Actually, she knew exactly how he did it because once or twice he'd turned that smile on her and it was darn hard to resist.

Even Tatiana had a shy smile for him as he asked if he could take a few photographs. He snapped the two women together, one of Cruella – Mirela – alone, and twenty quick ones of Tatiana with her violin raised to her chin in what Bernadette was beginning to call her 'Degas' dancer' pose.

He was right to be quick because Mirela soon tired of having her protégé be the focus of his attention.

"She must get back," she said in that heavy, central European accent that only added to her crazy villainess mystique.

"Could we set up an interview for tomorrow?" Bernadette asked as Mirela waited impatiently while Tatiana put her exquisite instrument away in its velvet lined, hard shell case.

Mirela thought for a moment, then asked with narrowed eyes, "Who did you say you were working for?"

"Strad Magazine," Rocky put in smoothly. That was a new one for Bernadette, but knowing they would try to sell stories to other magazines as well as to *Let's Travel*, she played along.

Rocky's answer seemed to please Mirela. "Certainly," she gushed. "Will tomorrow morning work for you? Our rooms at the hotel?" She turned to Rocky with a predatory smile. "And maybe you will take more photographs?"

He returned her smile, but put a hand on Bernadette's lower back and said, "Looking forward to it. We'd better get back out there. Bernadette?"

As they moved away, Bernadette chuckled. "I think she likes you."

Rocky gave a mock shudder. "Let's get out of here. I was afraid she was going to eat me alive."

Bernadette grinned. "You can't help it if you're so darn attractive to older women."

"Hey," he said, feigning insult. "She's not that old. And could be quite attractive – if she weren't so scary."

Bernadette shook her head, the smug smile still on her face. "If you say so."

Rocky steered her through the thinning crowd. "I set up a meeting with Jay and his handler, too, for later this evening. I hope that's okay."

"Perfect. Since we have appointments to interview them both, let's hope Tatiana and Jay both make it to the next round."

Chapter 21

An hour later, they found seats in a busy restaurant down the street from the venue.

"I'm starved," Rocky said.

Bernadette scanned the menu. "I'm hungry too. Everything looks delicious. Oh! *Parmigiano di melanzane*–that's eggplant, isn't it? Or gnocchi with sage in blackened butter. It's so hard to decide. It all sounds so good."

"You could get both," Rocky said. "Gnocchi is a *primo*, a first course. You could have the eggplant for the *secondo*."

"Tempting. But so is the *Quatro Formaggi Pizza*. I wonder what four cheeses they use."

"Parmesan, Mozzarella, Asiago and I'm not sure what the fourth cheese would be."

Unable to decide, in the end they chose to share all three dishes.

When the waiter left with their order, Rocky sat back in his chair. "I don't know much about classical music, but I wasn't surprised that Jay and Tatiana made it into the next round."

Bernadette nodded. "I thought they would too. And Angelo –"

Rocky grinned. "I'm not saying it's rigged, but the Italian *had* to make it through."

Bernadette nodded. "I was surprised Cordelia made it, but what do I know? I'm glad Una got through, though. She's a firecracker." She grinned. "I wasn't sure about the last two spots, but the German and Swiss contestants did play well."

Rocky nodded. "The next round is a new piece."

Bernadette winced. "The same piece played seven times."

Rocky pressed his lips together. "I'm thinking we could –"

"Skip it?" Bernadette finished hopefully.

He nodded and breathed a sigh of relief.

The waiter returned with a bottle of mineral water and another of Valpolicella just as Bernadette's cell phone rang. She glanced quickly at Rocky, paused a beat, then dug it out of her bag. Her son Colin had called when they'd been in Mexico, so Rocky figured it was him.

He smiled. "Say 'hi' from me."

Bernadette shot him a puzzled look over her sunglasses, then she pushed them up her nose with her pointer finger until they hid her eyes. Slinging one arm over the back of the chair and crossing her legs to the side, she turned her back to him and answered in a low voice. "Hi. Yes ... Everything's fine. ... My flights were fine ... Yes. Very nice."

Strange way to talk to her twelve-year-old son, but he supposed she could be talking anyone. The smile froze on his face at the thought of who else would be making an overseas call to check on how she was doing.

"Look, I can't talk right now. I'll call you later...Okay. Bye." She closed the phone, dropped it into her purse and turned back to face him.

She didn't offer any explanation – and why should she? – but who the hell was she talking to if it wasn't her son?

He kept a tight smile on his face, but couldn't stop himself from asking, "Your son?"

The high points of her cheeks flushed pink. She cleared her throat. "No, actually, it was Martin."

"Martin." His voice dropped, the repetition an unstated question. Somehow he managed to keep his face immobile. As stone.

"Ah, yes. I told you about him, didn't I? I'm sure I did. He's my...we've been seeing each other."

Now Rocky's eyebrows arched to his hairline. "Seeing each other?" He forced his brows down and attempted to smile. "Great." She hadn't been seeing anyone when they were in Mexico. Not that he knew of. But that was six months ago. "How long have you been, seeing each other."

She thought. "Mmmm. Five and a half months?"

Really? So right when he had been breaking up with Samantha – not that he did that *because* of Bernadette, but even so – right when he'd been breaking up with Samantha, she was picking up with this guy. "So, what does *Martin* do?"

"He works at the university."

"A professor?"

"No." She paused. "In accounting."

Accounting. Rocky wasn't able to stop a slow, smug smile.

Bernadette raised an accusatory eyebrow. "And how is Samantha?"

Rocky's eyes narrowed. All right. So he might not have told her he'd broken up with Samantha. Their emails had been friendly, but short. After all, it was business. But every time Bernadette's name popped up in his inbox, he'd registered a charge. Guess it wasn't reciprocal.

He leaned back, crossed his legs nonchalantly and said, "Oh, Sam and I broke up. A while ago." It had, in fact, been the week after he returned from Mexico. He waved his hand and said, "It was a long time coming."

Bernadette's eyes widened then narrowed thoughtfully. "Really. I didn't know."

Suddenly he wondered if telling her would have made a difference to her. Enough of a difference that she might not have taken up with Martin.

"So, is there someone new?" she asked casually. Too casually? Or was that wishful thinking?

He looked her straight in the eye. "Nope. No one new."

She frowned, briefly, squinting and twisting her mouth to the side. But it was over in a flash.

"I see," she said, and just then the waiter arrived with the pizza. Bernadette's attention shifted and, with a grin, she lifted a piece, put it on a plate and offered it to Rocky. Then she took a piece for herself, dripping with four cheeses, and dug in, Martin obviously forgotten.

Chapter 22

When they'd paid for their lunch, Bernadette asked, "Are we going to drive to Mondo Musica?"

"Not worth it. The parking lot will be packed. Besides, there's a shuttle bus from the Duomo piazza to the arena," Rocky said, finishing his espresso. "You done?" Not waiting for an answer, he stood up. "Let's go."

Bernadette chugged her coffee and gathered her things together. When Rocky was in work mode, manners went out the window. He was wearing his working gear, a safari style jacket with plenty of pockets for camera equipment, the straps of two camera cases making an X across his chest, and he carried a walking stick that he used as a monopod when a tripod was too cumbersome.

The sun was riding high in the sky, its warm fingers reaching into the narrow streets. As accomplished as the young contestants were, it felt good to be outside after a morning spent listening to the violin competition in the stuffy hall. They didn't have to wait long in front of the Duomo for the shuttle, but by the time the bus arrived they'd been joined by a few other people. Luckily, the square was the first stop on the route because the bus emptied when it pulled up and they were able to get a seat.

The arena wasn't far. They could probably have walked there in the time it took the bus to wind through old streets and impossibly narrow lanes to the half dozen stops on its route. These included the violin museum, the newer Continental Hotel on the edge of town, then back into the old center to the archeological museum, which Bernadette had put on her trip itinerary. By the time they reached the train station there was standing room only in the bus. The last stop was *la Fiera di Cremona,* the modern arena on the edge of town where they'd been to the opening the night before.

Cars poured into the large parking lot, but their bus skirted the congestion and dropped them conveniently at the front entrance where the flags on the flagpoles snapped briskly in the warm wind. The doors were just opening and they joined the press of people, all trying to be the first inside. Again, using the participant passes from Mia, they breezed through the VIP turnstile and soon were walking down the first long aisle of booths.

The red and black backdrops supplied by the festival lent a dramatic tone. Rocky pulled out his camera and was taking advantage of the sparse early crowd to get clean shots of various displays. Bernadette was amazed at the scale of the event. There must have been hundreds of exhibitors in the huge arena. Many were violin makers, some with modest displays of only a few instruments, usually violins, but some also displayed violas, cellos, and the odd double bass. Big name factories like the Japanese Yamaha and Suzuki, and the Romania factory HORA, displayed shiny instruments in slick, corner booths, and private dealers from all over Europe had instruments, old and new, safely stashed in glass cases. Bernadette spotted bow makers, guitar makers, and even a display featuring a gleaming grand piano. As well, there were suppliers of everything a luthier could need: bridges, strings, pegs, tools, and wood. Early-bird violin makers were already combing through double-sized booths full of instrument wood from central Europe.

Excitement swirled in the air as Bernadette and Rocky strolled down aisle after rapidly-filling aisle as people streamed into the exhibition space. Students and professional players began trying out instruments, sampling the wares of the makers and dealers, shooting incredibly complicated runs and riffs into the air before picking up another violin and playing the same thing all over again. The noise level quickly grew to a cacophony of sound until finally Bernadette gave Rocky the "time-out" hand signal, raising her pinky and bringing an imaginary cup to her lips.

Rocky nodded and led the way to a crowded coffee bar in one corner of the arena. Italian style, they paid in one spot, then took their ticket to a barista behind the counter who made their drinks. Then you found a spot at one of the tables to drink it, standing up. Bernadette soon saw that this wasn't a relaxing social cup of coffee. It was a pit stop for serious vendors and players before hurling themselves back into the fray.

While she waited for her turn at the cash, she noticed most people ordered espresso, dumped in a packet of sugar, then downed it like a shot, in one gulp. When they got to the cash register, that's what Rocky ordered, so she decided to try it, too. It was sticky and sweet and went straight to her blood stream like a shot of whisky, but instead of muddying her brain, she suddenly felt clear headed and ready to get back to work.

Directly across from the café, plastered in block letters on an arch above the entry of a big corner booth, was the name FANUCCI. Bernadette recognized the name of the violin dealer Hamish was drinking with the night of his death.

Without any discussion, Bernadette and Rocky finished their drinks, crossed the aisle, and walked under the arch into Fanucci's sumptuous booth.

Chapter 23

The floor of Fanucci's booth was covered with multiple Persian carpets that overlapped in a haphazard pattern, and the walls were decorated with glass cases displaying instruments, each with a brass nameplate of the maker beneath. No prices, Bernadette noted. Dates beneath the instruments went as far back as the seventeenth and eighteenth centuries, hinting that their prices were bound to be astronomical. Rocky had said Hamish had told him that a violin could go for millions of dollars. It was thrilling to think that one of the instruments she'd see today might be worth that much.

The names of the Italian makers and cities rolled off her tongue: Pietro Anselmo, Bergamo Rovetta – she loved the Italian language! – and one by Carlo Bergonzi, *circa* 1740, obviously the star of the instruments out on display. She was dying to hold it. She *needed* to hold it. Her hand reached out and caressed the glass separating her from the violin. A pulse tingled through her fingertips and up her arm, the feeling rolling through her like a drug.

Suddenly she realized where she was and how it must look. She pulled her hand away and shook her head to snap herself out of it. Then she dug a pad and pen out of her purse. Better to keep her hands busy.

Rocky came and stood beside her. He took pictures of the violin in the case without a flash, using his monopod to brace the camera.

A young man dressed in a slick Italian suit approached and said, "*Buon giorno.* Is there something I can help you with? Something you'd like to see?"

His English was particularly good, and Bernadette could see why Fanucci had hired him. She took a business card out of her purse and handed it to him, garnering a surprised look from Rocky. She'd ordered them on a whim a few weeks before when news of the job first came her way, and now she was glad she had. If nothing else, it made her feel like a real writer, which, she reminded herself, she was. Even if this was only her second assignment.

The young man looked at the card and nodded, then took it to Fanucci who sat behind a heavy antique desk in the corner of the opulent booth. A rotund man in a blue suit that was a bit too tight and a bit too bright, his arms crossed on his chest, he glanced at the business card, then looked Bernadette and Rocky over like the salesman he was and motioned for them to approach the desk.

Arrogant, Bernadette thought. Like a potentate greeting a petitioner. All he needed was a robe and a staff.

"Alessandro Fanucci," he said, the name rolling off his tongue like honey as he half-rose from his chair and held out a pudgy be-ringed hand to shake, first to Bernadette then to Rocky. "Please, have a seat." He indicated the two antique chairs set in front of the desk for consultations.

Bernadette smiled pleasantly and, sensing this man would respond to compliments, said, "Signore Fanucci, it is so nice to meet you. We have been hearing your name ever since we arrived in Cremona."

"Nothing bad, I hope," he joked, obviously please by the flattery.

She flared her eyes. "Oh, no, not at all. I've heard you are the man to go to in Cremona – perhaps in the world – to have an instrument authenticated." She wondered if she had gone too far with the "in the world" part, but maybe not if his widening smile was anything to go by.

"*One* of the foremost world experts, perhaps," he demurred, running a hand through his slicked-back hair. "Why, do you have an instrument you need authenticated?"

"No. My partner and I are working on an article for a magazine," she continued. "If you have a moment, I'd like to ask you a few questions."

Fanucci's eyes narrowed, and he glanced over her shoulder at the empty booth behind her. "Perhaps, a moment, *si,* but I expect to be busy very soon."

"Of course." She poised her pen above her pad. "How exactly do you authenticate an instrument?"

"It is not an exact science," he said. "It is the accumulation of years of experience studying thousands of instruments, talking to experts in the field."

"And where better than in the home of Stradivari himself?" Bernadette added.

"Precisely."

"So, it is mostly experience? Is there no science involved?"

"Sometimes we use dendrology on the wood – the science of examining tree rings to determine where and when the tree grew. It is something like looking at a tree's DNA. But that is extremely expensive and rarely used – only in cases where the age of an expensive violin is under dispute. Generally, people trust my determination."

"Of course," Bernadette said quickly. "You are the expert. And how much do you charge for your services?" she asked, looking up expectantly.

"The base price is one thousand Euros." He closed his eyes and made a flicking gesture with his hand. "I do not wish to waste my time on instruments of lower value. But the final price depends."

"On what?" Bernadette pressed.

"On the value of the violin, and how much work is involved."

"I saw you at the hotel the other night," Rocky interrupted. "With the Scottish man who was murdered. Amos Ballantyne."

Fanucci's eyes flashed to Rocky, suddenly wary, but only for a second before sliding into an appropriately neutral expression. "Signore Ballantyne. Yes, I was sorry to hear he met with such an unfortunate accident. Was he an acquaintance of yours?"

Calling a direct shot to the chest an "accident" was harshly evasive, but perhaps the details were not common knowledge. Rocky didn't pursue the point.

"He was," Rocky said. "I met him in London years ago. I was surprised to see him here, but he always was a keen collector, if not a particularly good violinist." Rocky gave an equally appropriate sad smile. "Was he going to buy a violin from you?"

Fanucci gave a vague shrug. "We were talking. He wanted something by one of the grand masters of our golden age. I was not able to help him. They do not often come onto the market." He paused for a moment, looking over their heads into the booth.

"I am sorry, but now I must see to my customers," he finished smoothly, standing to indicate the interview was over.

Finished for now, Bernadette thought, also rising.

As she shook his hand, she tried to tune in to any uncomfortable feelings. Vibrations. Anything. But no. Nothing. Never, it seemed, when she asked for clarity.

Thanking him for his time, she added, "I hope it's okay if we come to you if we have any more questions regarding authentication, since you are the expert."

Fanucci dipped his head in an imperious gesture that she decided to take as a *yes*.

Chapter 24

Bernadette could have sworn she felt the chill of Fanucci's eyes on her back as she and Rocky walked away from the booth. But within moments the noise, the colour, the general chaos of the music fair was enough of a distraction that she went back to making notes on her surroundings. The booths were all either black, red, or a combination of both, very baroque for the twenty first century. Some were small, a simple table or a case with a single instrument, while others blossomed to multiple booths strung together for larger companies and established makers or dealers.

The noise level had risen considerably since their arrival, and now the aisles were even more crowded with people of all nationalities. She heard English spoken, with both North American and British accents, German, a variety of Eastern European languages she could not tell apart, and Spanish. As well, she recognized Japanese and a surprising amount of Chinese. And, of course, rising above it all, Italian, in highly animated discussions about, she assumed, the merits of the instruments. The Italians all seemed to be experts. This was their party, and they were enjoying it.

The pandemonium of sound billowed over everything, with instruments being played with gusto in almost every booth. She wondered how anyone could decide on an instrument to buy in this bedlam. But many seemed eager to try, picking up and trying one instrument after another.

Bernadette's head began to spin and she felt the first panicky adrenalin rush of claustrophobia: a sparking at the edges of her vision; an increased blurring of focus. Then she felt Rocky take her arm. He seemed to sense when she was in trouble, but this time, unlike his distain when they'd been in Mexico, it felt like a helpful hand in a difficult moment.

He guided her to a long, triple booth where she saw Stephano Passero, in a beige cotton shop coat over a clean white shirt and scruffy jeans, holding court with a group of eager Japanese men in suits and ties. The back wall of the booth was hung with two rows of violins, the tags beneath them showing the names of makers. Their prices ranged in the tens of thousands of Euros. It was vibrant, exciting, quite different in mood from Fanucci's booth.

Rocky's cousin Mia came forward to greet them. She was dressed in slim black pants and a black tunic. Her *Partecipante* name tag hung around her neck. Although she was on duty, she seemed pleased to see them.

"Ciao," she said, exchanging air kisses with them both.

"Whose violins are these?" Bernadette asked, indicating the instruments hanging in their end of the booth.

"The apprentices made these. Passero always has apprentices. He likes to help young people get a start in the business." She smiled proudly. "I am an apprentice too."

"Are any of these yours?" Rocky asked.

"Not yet. Maybe next year. I am the low man on the ladder, the most recent apprentice. I am lucky he took me on while I am still at *la scuola*."

"Ah, yes, the *scuola*," Bernadette said. She had read about the violin makers school, set up by Mussolini to revive the violin trade in the city at a time when it had almost died out. Now, eighty years later, it was still going strong.

"I graduate in the spring and after will become a full apprentice here. Then I will be allowed to work on my own violins. I can give you a tour of the shop sometime."

"That would be great." Rocky said.

"Which are Passero's violins?" Bernadette asked.

Mia led them over to the other end of the booth where the Japanese delegation had moved on and Passero stood, arms folded on his chest, surveying the crowd. Rocky greeted him more formally than he had Mia, calling him *maestro*, as befitted his stature as a master violinmaker. Bernadette was beginning to realize that the violin world, like much of Italy, was a community steeped in tradition.

Bernadette followed Rocky's lead, keeping her greeting polite, then, with Mia translating, asked him a few questions. At Rocky's suggestion, Passero posed for a picture with Mia, as if showing her one of his violins. Within minutes, though, a couple walked into the booth with their university-aged daughter and Passero turned his attention to them. The Mondo Musica long weekend, while exciting, was not turning out to be the best time to interview makers and dealers.

"I'd like to talk with him more sometime," Bernadette said to Mia as they moved away.

"There will be time," Mia assured her. "When the fair is over."

It sounded like it would be a busy two days at the end of their trip if they were to interview everyone she wanted to talk to before they flew home.

Just then an impromptu concert started in the next booth, a trio with bass, violin, and guitar playing Gypsy jazz reminiscent of the famous Roma musician Django Reinhardt. Bernadette and Rocky watched the performance with the gathering crowd and applauded robustly when it was over.

"Now, that's more my kind of music," Rocky said, his lips close to Bernadette's ear. She knew it was to be heard over the noise of the crowd, but she still felt a rush at his closeness.

When the music stopped, they said their goodbyes to Mia – Passero being occupied with a customer.

The general noise level in the arena had continued to increase to the point that, even though Rocky was right beside her, he had to shout to be heard. "Enough for now?"

Laughing, she nodded, covered her ears with her hands and headed for the door.

Chapter 25

As they forged their way through the crowd toward the exit, Rocky and Bernadette stumbled upon another impromptu performance, this time at Fanucci's booth. The tune was familiar, and the line of music that drifted out through the archway sent a shiver down Bernadette's spine.

She stopped in her tracks and, after a few steps, Rocky came back and stood by her side.

"Who is it?" he asked.

She shook her head. She couldn't see, but since they were playing a Bach Partita, she felt sure it was one of the Crown contestants.

Shifting so that she could see through the screen of violins hanging on the glass wall of Fanucci's booth, Bernadette caught a glimpse of the player. It was Jay, his eyes closed, body swaying, lost in the music.

Then she caught a flash of color amongst the more somber tones of Fanucci's booth – Mirela Florescu's fluorescent pink coat, and Tatiana was by her side.

Jay seemed under the spell of the music, and when he finished playing appeared surprised that an audience had assembled in the corridor. He gave a quick nod toward the appreciative crowd and turned to Fanucci. The dealer moved in close, keeping their conversation private. If he was trying to sell Jay on the instrument, it didn't look like he'd have to try very hard. The young man cradled the violin possessively, like a baby, in the crook of one arm and ran his other hand lovingly over its sensuous curves.

Bernadette felt Rocky's arm slide around her waist and pull her close. With his lips by her ear, he said, "I wish I could hear what Fanucci is saying."

Bernadette nodded.

Jay handed the violin back to Fanucci with obvious regret and watched as the dealer put it in an hard-shell case that was open on his desk. Jay turned toward the open arch, casting one last longing glance at the violin.

Even before he had left the booth, Mirela took her charge by the arm and pulled Tatiana over to Fanucci's desk. The dealer stood and shook her offered hand, looking with interest at Tatiana when Mirela introduced her. They seemed to be talking about the violin, too, but Bernadette noticed Fanucci didn't invite them to sit. At length, he grudgingly took the violin out of the case and handed it to Tatiana. As she studied it, Mirela fidgeted at her side, leaning forward to look first at the violin, then to speak excitedly to Fanucci. His eyes narrowed and his lips pressed together under her barrage of words.

Slowly Tatiana lifted the instrument to her shoulder, took a moment to settle it under her chin, then reached for the bow that was on the desk and began to play.

It was not the piece she had played at the competition. It sounded more like a mournful folk tune. Bernadette stiffened. It was the melody she'd heard in the square with Rocky the first night, immediately before Hamish's murder. A tingle ran up her arms and the hubbub of the arena receded as the music surrounded her.

Then suddenly she felt Rocky's hands on her shoulders, shaking her gently, whispering her name in her ear. Her eyes flew open. His face was mere inches away.

The music had stopped and the audience who had gathered burst into applause. She didn't know how long she had been missing in action, under the spell.

Fanucci, too, seemed surprised by the power of Tatiana's playing, but still possessively retrieved the instrument from her and returned it to the case, albeit with increased respect.

Mirela started talking again and watched intently while Fanucci carefully latched the lid. He tried the locks to check they'd caught, then placed the case in a wooden cabinet behind the desk and purposefully turned the key which he then secreted in an inside pocket of his vest.

Rocky took Bernadette's hand, breaking into her thoughts, and hitched his head toward the exit. They wove through the crowd until they emerged into the warm, gusty afternoon sunshine.

The shuttle bus stop was crowded and as they stood waiting in line, Rocky took the opportunity to scroll through the pictures on his camera. "Everyone seems interested in that violin," he observed.

Peering over his shoulder at the camera screen, Bernadette could see he was looking at pictures of Jay and Fanucci, taken while Jay was giving his impromptu concert, and afterward while he and Fanucci talked.

"It looks like Jay has his eye on that violin," Bernadette said.

"I wonder what kind of backing he has?" Rocky mused.

"Looks like an entitled rich kid to me."

Rocky tipped his head to the side. "But is he *that* rich? Those violins can go for hundreds of thousands. Sometimes millions."

She shook her head. "I don't know. Maybe he has a rich backer."

"Possibly. But I don't think Tatiana could afford something like that. I don't think she has that kind of backing."

"Mirela looked like the one who was really interested," Bernadette said. She paused, remembering the feeling that had washed over her as Jay, and particularly Tatiana, played Fanucci's violin. "I wonder..."

Rocky cocked his head. "Wonder what?"

Bernadette blushed. "I had a feeling while they were playing. Similar to the feeling I had in the square the night Hamish was murdered. Could this be the violin Hamish was trying to buy?"

Chapter 26

When Bernadette got back to her room, the hotel phone was ringing. She picked up the receiver and sat on the bed. "*Pronto,*" she said into the handset, pleased to be able to try out the Italian greeting.

"Ciao!" It was Jen, her editor at *Let's Travel* magazine.

Bernadette smiled at the sound of her old friend's voice. Then she winced at the thought of having to tell her about the murder.

"How are things going?" Jen asked.

"Okay. Great! Cremona is hopping with the contest and Mondo Musica. We've done a few interviews already and have more lined up."

There was a pause on the other end of the line, then Jen said, "I heard there was a murder in town. I hope this won't interfere with you getting your story."

Bernadette closed her eyes and bit her lip, searching for an answer that would satisfy Jen. But she had nothing, except the truth.

"Well, as a matter of fact, Rocky did know the...deceased." There was silence on the line, so Bernadette stumbled on. "But of course we had nothing to do with the murder. It was a coincidence and happened right after we got here and they met. Not met up," she amended quickly. "Just met, by chance, at the hotel bar."

Better to stop here. Her explanation wasn't helping.

"How is Rocky handling it?" Jen asked.

"You know Rocky. Rolling with it. Determined not to get involved."

"Mm-hmmm," Jen responded noncommittally. Bernadette could virtually see her thinking, rolling the rubber ball she kept on her desk around and around with her palm. "Well, be sure you keep it that way." Jen paused for a moment, and Bernadette was relieved when she changed the subject. "How does Martin feel about you going to Italy for the week with Rocky?"

This was not much better. She had told Jen about Martin when they had caught up before the trip. But now that she was here, it was a subject Bernadette was trying not to think about.

"He's a little miffed."

Jen laughed. "Miffed?"

Bernadette sighed. It was the most vehement response she'd ever had from him. He was such an even-tempered guy. Which, she reminded herself, was what she liked about him.

"I know, he's not the most exciting guy in the world," she said. "But he's dependable, which is more than I can say for Colin's father."

"When was the last time you saw *him*?" Jen asked.

"Colin's father? Three years ago. He showed up a month late for Colin's birthday with an extravagant gift, a drone that I wasn't sure Colin should even have. The kid was

only 8 years old! They spent two fun-filled days at the park eating ice cream and flying the darn thing, then he announced that was all the time he had and *bam!* – he was gone. Off to a dig in Uzbekistan! He said he'd be back."
Sure he would.

"Has Colin met Martin yet?"

"Not yet. It's still early. I don't want Colin getting any ideas."

"And what about Rocky?" Jen asked in an annoyingly insinuating tone. "You two seemed to hit it off in Mexico."

Bernadette huffed an embarrassed laugh. "I'm not sure I'd call what we went through in Mexico 'hitting it off'."

"He broke up with his girlfriend right after he got back, so I thought...But I guess not."

Right after they got back? Bernadette put that aside to think about later. She was grateful when Jen changed to a safer subject. "Well I'm glad you're on track with the story. Just keep it that way." And on that note, Jen ended the call.

Bernadette groaned and flopped back on the bed. *Dependable.* Was that the best thing she could think of to say about Martin? She came back from the week in Mexico with Rocky all fired up and decided it was time to start dating. And okay, it was Rocky who'd gotten her motor revving again, but he'd been in a relationship and, equally important, they had a professional partnership she did not want to jeopardize.

And Martin was nice. *Very* nice. Although she had to admit, not very exciting.

But was excitement what she wanted in her life right now? A slow grin crossed her face as she thought back to the wild ride in Paola's boat down the river, then the scooter ride across the fields, and the crazy ride back to town in the rattletrap Fiat. Life with Rocky was always exciting.

When Martin picked her up for a date it was in his grey Toyota Corolla. Her smile seeped away, and she rubbed her face with both hands. She felt like she had a split personality. She had her – all right, say it – boring mom-life, dating Martin, a perfectly nice man, and working at the university transcribing field notes for her old professor who – at sixty-five! – was still out in the field every break he got, making discoveries the archeological world couldn't wait to hear about. That comparison, his opportunities compared to hers, had grated for years. But now, with this job with the magazine, she was suddenly leaving that life behind to fly off to exotic countries, meeting exciting people and having *adventures* – she hoped for at least one adventure on this trip – with the most exciting man she'd ever met *who had broken up with his girlfriend right after their trip to Mexico!*

She hit her forehead with the heel of her hand.

That exhilarating week in Mexico with Rocky had opened her up to the possibility of a new relationship. And a new, more exciting life. Although obviously she hadn't thought it would be with Rocky. The man was a loose cannon, liable to get them into all sorts of trouble.

Yes, a devilish voice whispered within, *but it would be a wild ride.*

Chapter 27

B ernadette put her conversation with Jen out of her mind, at least the part about Rocky, and got to work on her story notes. Two hours later she stretched, grabbed her bag, intending to meet Rocky at the lobby restaurant. She had no sooner stepped out into the hallway when a shriek echoed down the dim corridor.

She raced toward the sound and found Tatiana's door wide open. The young woman stood inside the room, hands pressed to her cheeks, eyes wide in horror. On the floor at her feet, white tissue paper frothed out of an open box.

Bernadette rushed to her side and put a hand on the girl's arm. "What is it?"

Before Tatiana could answer, Mirela stormed into the room, fur trimmed edges of her long black sweater aflutter, and pushed Bernadette aside.

Mirela began a tirade in Romanian aimed at the girl, and Tatiana burst into tears, covering her face with her hands. Mirela made a dismissive gesture with one hand as she reached down with the other to retrieve the box. She parted the tissue and made what could only have been a Romanian curse.

She wheeled on Bernadette and verbally attacked. "Are you responsible? Did you give her this?"

Bernadette backed up, right into Rocky who, hearing the uproar, had appeared at the door. His hand landed reassuringly on her shoulder.

"No," she said. "I don't even know what's *in* the box."

Mirela thrust the offender under her nose and Bernadette saw it was full of thin shards of wood, splinters really, and curling wires. Then she saw a neck and a scroll. A violin, in a hundred pieces. She sucked in a horrified breath.

Suddenly she had a terrible thought. "Is this your violin?"

Mirela picked up a shard and looked at it disdainfully. "Not one of ours. Not a good violin. Just a factory instrument."

Tatiana rubbed her hands together and Bernadette could see she was rattled. She spoke to Mirela in Romanian, gesturing wildly, pointing out into the hall every few words, then back to the box with the shattered violin. She must have vindicated Bernadette because Mirela turned away from her charge and said to Bernadette, "No matter. No harm done."

Rocky cut in. "Who brought it?"

Tatiana took a deep breath to calm herself, and switched to English. "A man in a uniform. Maybe a hotel employee?"

"Just now?" Rocky persisted.

Tatiana nodded, glancing in horror – or fear – at the box in Mirela's hand as if it was, or had recently been, alive.

"We'll see what we can find out," Rocky offered, taking Bernadette by the arm and leading her back out into the corridor.

Bernadette tried to smile reassuringly at Tatiana over her shoulder as she left. The girl looked at her woefully, but Mirela only nodded briefly to them in dismissal then firmly closed the door.

Rocky gave Bernadette's arm a nudge, propelling her toward the elevator.

"Tatiana looked scared," Bernadette said as she punched the down button.

"I don't blame her," Rocky replied. "It was a threat. Or designed as a curse. Romanians are often very superstitious. In some places, curses are still a way of life."

"It certainly upset Tatiana, but why target her specifically?"

Rocky shrugged. "She's one of the top contenders to win the competition. Maybe someone is trying to shake her up. Stop her from playing her best."

"Who would do that?"

"Someone who really wants to win."

They approached the front desk and asked the clerk if any parcels had recently been delivered. He said that no parcels had arrived for Signorina Tatiana Ciobanu, but that a man in a courier uniform had come in recently and gone directly upstairs. Rocky got the name of the company and thanked the clerk, who by this time was apologizing profusely, obviously worried about reprisals.

"That was easy," Bernadette said softly as they turned away.

"Probably afraid he'll lose his job," Rocky said. "Security is pretty lax considering how many valuable instruments are in the rooms upstairs."

They crossed the foyer to the restaurant where half the tables were taken and the clink of glasses and the murmur of voices filled the air. They ordered cappuccinos, then sat in silence, each lost in their thoughts.

Bernadette watched Rocky survey the people in the room. "What are you looking for?"

"Just checking to see if anyone besides Tatiana looks particularly jumpy."

Bernadette scanned the room. It was quieter than the previous day. Most of the patrons were the remaining Crown contestants and their chaperones. "They are probably all nervous. The second round of the contest is tomorrow, and at that point half of the remaining contestants will be eliminated."

Rocky suddenly stood up. "Nothing to see here. Let's find somewhere else to eat."

Chapter 28

They found a small family restaurant two blocks from the hotel, a place they had passed before, but during the day the shutters had been closed. Tonight the lights were on and a simple handwritten menu hung at the entrance. When they opened the door, Bernadette almost swooned as tantalizing aromas washed over her.

Because they planned to interview Jay that evening, dinner was not the usual prolonged event it often is in Italy. Still, her share of the bottle of wine was more than Bernadette usually drank so when they exited back onto the street, she welcomed the cool evening air that cleared her head on the short walk to the hotel.

Rocky was unusually silent over dinner so she suspected he was thinking about the progress in the investigation into Hamish's death. As an ex-police detective, he would want to see his friend's murderer caught, but she hoped they could leave the investigation to the Italian police, get on with their own job, their story for the magazine, and not be drawn in any further.

"Jay's good," she said, hoping to distract him. "He'd be my pick for one of the top three. What do you think?"

"I agree. I'm not an expert, but he's a confident player. His stage presence alone would add marks, whether the judges want to admit it or not. We should be sure to get an interview with that judge Roth again somewhere along the way."

"One morning? Over breakfast?" Bernadette suggested wistfully, hoping to get at least one more fresh, farm breakfast.

"I'd vote for Tatiana, too," she continued. "She has that wistful air about her. You feel the sadness in her soul when she plays."

"You seem to, anyway," Rocky said, as they walked up the front steps to the hotel.

She gave a sheepish smile. "I don't really play the violin anymore, but my fingers twitch a little when I watch them play."

They knocked on Jay's door and before he could answer, his teacher Gloria slipped out of the room next door and joined them in the hall. She was small and delicate, and unlike many of the other chaperones, seemed like the less dominant partner in the Jay/Gloria duo.

She smiled pleasantly and shook both their hands. "Hello. I'm Gloria, Jay's teacher. We met the other night at the bar."

"Of course," Bernadette said, reintroducing herself and Rocky.

"Thank you for coming. So nice of you both to interview Jay like this," Gloria said as Jay swung open his room door.

'Room' was an understatement. Unlike Bernadette's own small, basic single room, Jay had a suite, a modest sitting room with, she could see, two adjoining rooms. One was obviously the room from which Gloria had emerged.

"This is very nice," Bernadette said as Jay ushered them inside. "Do all of the contestants get suites?"

"No. I thought there might be press. The sitting room is much better for interviews than sitting on the bed or in the noisy bar, don't you think?"

"It certainly is." Then she couldn't help but ask, "Did your parents come with you?"

"No, they were too busy. Gloria is my teacher this year, so she accompanied me." He walked to a collection of wine and water bottles on the side table. "May I get you a drink?"

The mother in Bernadette lifted her head again, wondering if he was even old enough to drink.

"I'll just have water, please," she said quickly.

"Me too," Rocky added, getting his camera out of the bag.

When they were settled, Bernadette began. "We saw the concert. You seem amazingly comfortable on stage. How old are you?"

"Nineteen," Jay said, handing them their water. Then he sat on the small sofa with Gloria, resting his arm along the back and something about their body language seemed to confirm the fact that there was more to their relationship than student and teacher. But, she reminded herself, that was their business and had nothing to do with the article.

"Have you performed much?"

Jay launched into a veritable CV of his performances with smaller orchestras in the north-eastern states near the small Massachusetts town where he grew up. "I go to The Eastman School of Music now." He paused for a moment as if expecting a response, and while Bernadette thought she might have heard of it, she wasn't sure.

Gloria filled the gap. "Eastman is one of the premiere music schools in the United States."

Jay shot her a haughty glance. "In the world."

"I see," Bernadette said, trying to infuse her voice with enough expression to satisfy Jay. "And it's in…?"

"Rochester," Gloria said.

"It must be difficult to get in," Bernadette said.

"Only thirteen percent of candidates who apply get in," Jay announced proudly. "I was top in my class last year."

"Really," Bernadette said with feeling, scribbling a note of that in her book, trying to hide her growing annoyance at Jay's bravado. "So, I guess winning the Cremona Crown would be a feather in your cap? How do you think it would change the trajectory of your career?"

"I could tour for a year, probably more, on the Crown," Jay said, a disturbing note of avarice in his voice.

"We saw you play in Fanucci's booth at Mondo Musica earlier today," Rocky cut in.

"Yes. I'm trying to trade in my Bergonzi for something better. Something that would lift my performance to an even higher level. He has the most amazing Guarneri. Just came to light. It has been lost for half a century. Fanucci's the kind of dealer who people bring these special instruments to, and he let me play it! I'd give anything to own it."

Never having gotten to the level where she thought a better instrument would have made a significant impact on her playing, Bernadette asked, "Does the violin make that much difference?"

"For a superior player it can. But first I need to get my Bergonzi certified." He leaned forward earnestly, resting his elbows on his knees. "I bought it from a dealer in the States when I was accepted at Eastman, but it came without papers. It would be worth so much more if I could get papers from Fanucci."

"Fanucci?" Bernadette asked, glancing at Rocky as she scribbled the name.

"He's the most respected dealer in Cremona. His certification is accepted by dealers and players around the world. If he says it's a Bergonzi, no one will dispute it. I'm hoping he will take mine as a trade."

Bernadette glanced at Rocky again. Had he caught it too? The desperate note in Jay's voice, as if the provenance of his violin was in question. Gustaf Braun, the dealer from Munich, had questioned the honesty of some dealers and the authenticity of some violins attributed to famous makers. His comments suddenly made more sense. She could see now how selling papers to owners of violins of questionable background could be a lucrative racket. Especially if that same dealer could then resell said violin.

At this point, Gloria turned the interview back to Jay's performance, until finally Rocky stepped in with his camera. He set Jay up for a few moody shots, but the low indoor evening light was not conducive to the best photographs.

"Perhaps we could meet and take more pictures later," Rocky suggested. "When the light is better."

"Certainly," Jay said enthusiastically. Then he laughed. "When I win the Crown!"

Although that was exactly the kind of egotistical statement that was getting on Bernadette's nerves, she put as much enthusiasm as she could into her voice. "Definitely. Especially if you win the Crown."

Soon after that, Rocky packed up his gear and they said good night.

As they walked away from Jay's door, Rocky said, "Up for a drink?"

"Sure," Bernadette replied. "I need something to wash the taste of that interview out of my mouth. Have you ever met anyone so arrogant? And at his age."

Rocky grinned. "Yes, Mom."

She blushed, then laughed. "I can't help it. Jay's not all that much older than Colin. Such an ego! I'd love to see him taken down a notch. It would do him good."

Chapter 29

When they got back down to the ground floor, Bernadette assumed they would go into the hotel bar, but instead Rocky took her arm and gently steered her across the lobby and outside.

"Let's go somewhere else. Somewhere we can talk without being surrounded by Crown contestants. Although I guess the whole town is full of violin people this weekend."

"Isn't it always?" Bernadette asked as they walked the half-block to Duomo Piazza.

"Not always. They host a lot of other festivals here too. Most of them have to do with food and farming. The sausage festival, the tractor festival, The Cheese Under the Sky festival."

Bernadette laughed. "What's that?"

"It's put on by organic milk and cheese producers using milk from pasture raised cows. My uncle's farm belongs to that group. I'll take you out to the barn and introduce you to the cows next time we're there."

Bernadette snuck him a curious look. This Cremonese Rocky was different from the sometimes-arrogant world traveller she'd met in Mexico. He was warmer, more down to earth. She supposed that was the family influence. However, what did she really know about the man? The one week they'd spent together in Mexico had been wild and exciting – racing for their lives more than once through the jungle – but it was hardly a normal week. Even for a week on assignment.

As they turned the corner into the Piazza, Bernadette felt a flash of trepidation about returning to the scene of the murder, but the yellow police tape had been removed and the square looked and felt quite festive. It was Friday night and Mondo Musica was in town. Brightly lit tables were set out on the cobbles in front of a bar that tonight was open for the evening.

They grabbed seats at a vacant, black ironwork table. A reassuring hum of chatter in many languages came from fellow imbibers at other tables, everyone enjoying the balmy night air and the warm glow cast by the lights reflected off the medieval buildings around the square.

"Cremona is usually a sleepy farming town," Rocky explained. "It closes up early in the evening. But weekends when the festivals are on, places like this stay open and put out tables. It's nice to get out of the hotel bar. I mentioned to Niccolo that we might stop here."

They ordered drinks from a roving waiter and Bernadette went inside the bar to select a pastry from the brightly lit glass display case. It was hard to choose, but she finally settled on a gooey delight, asked for two forks, and returned to the table.

They took turns taking bites and as they finished, Niccolo joined them, shaking Rocky's hand and bending down to kiss Bernadette lightly on both cheeks. Tonight he seemed more like the affable cousin who'd picked Bernadette up at the airport and less like the formal police officer they'd met at the morgue. Only to be expected, she supposed, licking the last of the chocolate whipped cream off her fork.

He took an empty seat at their table.

"Any movement on the case?" Rocky asked.

After a pause, Niccolo said, "I'm afraid it is out of my hands. Comissario Grassi has ordered me onto another assignment."

Rocky's anger surfaced like molten lava. He banged his glass on the table. "Why?"

"The case has been moved to another department. The Financial Police and the Art Police have taken it over. Grassi is furious."

"The Art Police? For a homicide?" Bernadette asked in confusion.

"*Tutela del Patrimonio Culturale.* It's part of the *Carabinieri*, the Military Police, which deals with the protection of art and cultural patrimony. We call it the TPC for short."

"Why the Military Police?"

"Because Hamish was asking about violins," Niccolo explained patiently.

"Seriously? Military Police? I mean, I know violins can be worth a lot of money, but I don't get it. Why would the Military Police be involved?"

"Italians take their cultural artifacts very seriously," Niccolo said. "There are priceless artifacts on display everywhere, in churches, public buildings, even private homes. They are often found buried while excavating for new buildings. Theft of these artifacts is rampant. As we know, some collectors have no scruples about buying stolen artifacts.

"The TPC moved into our offices a few weeks ago – all very hush hush – and now they have taken over the case. Grassi seems as frustrated as I am. He is livid at having the case taken away from our department. It is an insult."

"Art police," Rocky repeated, trying to wrap his head around the tangled web that was the Italian police system. "Do they have superior jurisdiction?"

Niccolo paused for a beat, then shrugged. "Maybe."

Rocky blew out a frustrated breath. "So, you're off the case."

"We are all off the case."

They were all silent for a moment, then Niccolo said, "Sorry, *cugino*, I cannot do anything for you. My hands are tied."

Rocky tilted his head and rocked back in his chair, eyes narrow. "Maybe *you* can't..."

Niccolo studied his cousin in silence, then said, "There is nothing I can do. Officially. But you know I am here if you need me."

Rocky's lips formed a firm line. "*Grazie.*"

Bernadette looked from Niccolo to Rocky. Okay, she got it. Message received. Now it was up to them.

"There's one thing you should know, though," Niccolo added.

"And what's that?"

"Our enquiry has been about the death of Amos Ballantyne. The commissioner has not been using Hamish's real name in the local inquiry."

Rocky nodded and filed this information away. "You'll let me know if you hear they are making progress."

His cousin's stern countenance relaxed. "I will. There is nothing firm. Not yet. 'Amos' was supposedly looking to buy a violin. Did he play? Did he have money to buy an expensive instrument?"

Rocky shook his head. "Not that I knew of. But we had a funny relationship. We were friends in a war zone where we were both on assignment. I never knew what his real life was like." He looked thoughtfully at the glowing Duomo façade. "I always thought that *was* his real life."

After a minute, Niccolo said, "I did look at his work. Thanks for the tip."

Rocky grinned. "So you *are* still on the case."

Niccolo lifted one shoulder again. "Informally. He must have been researching something to do with the violin business to have come to town this week. But it could have been anything. Anyone. He was talking to people all around town. But most of the foreigners hadn't arrived yet for Mondo Musica – they were just rolling in that night – which makes me think it could have been someone local."

"Or someone who got here early," Rocky mused.

"It is all so hard to believe," Bernadette said. "The violin world seems so benign." Niccolo snorted a laugh, and she quickly added, "To an outsider." Then she pictured Hamish, lying on the cold stone under the portico fifty feet from where they now sat, and blew out a heartfelt sigh. "But I guess not."

"There's big money involved, and even bigger prestige," Niccolo said. "Some violin players have tremendous egos."

Her thoughts immediately turned to Jay. Their interview had made it clear that for the contestants of the Cremona Crown, the drive for prestige begins early. And Bernadette had a feeling that in cases like Tatiana's, the money involved would be more than welcome.

A woman walked up to their table and laid a hand on Niccolo's shoulder. She wore high heeled boots and a fashionable soft woollen poncho. Her long dark hair shone in the soft light of the square. "Ciao."

"Fillippina," Niccolo said, taking her hand from his shoulder and turning it over to kiss the palm. Bernadette suppressed a sigh. So smooth, so romantic. So Italian.

Rocky pulled a fourth chair from a nearby empty table for her, but Niccolo stood and said, "Sorry *cugino*, we have plans. But let's have dinner one night this weekend."

Rocky stood. "I'd like that. Then we can talk." He clasped his cousin in a hug, then Niccolo and Fillippina left, strolling arm in arm across the square.

Once they were alone, the quiet ambience of the square at night settled over them again. Bernadette mulled over the implications of what Niccolo had said. "I had the feeling Jay was hinting that his violin might not be all he says it is."

"You caught that too?"

She nodded. "He as much as said that if you paid enough you could get a certificate that said almost anything."

Rocky finished his drink. "I bet you could. And if you are looking for someone to do that, this would be the week."

"And the place."

After a beat, Bernadette asked, "Fanucci?"

Rocky nodded. "Could be."

When they had first sat down, the stones paving the square had still released heat stored from the afternoon sun, but now a chill was creeping in. Bernadette shivered. She suddenly felt an overwhelming wave of fatigue. She never acclimatized easily to time changes. It was only her second full day in Italy, and it had been a long one. She put her hand over her mouth to cover an uncontrollable yawn.

"Time to go?" Rocky asked.

She smiled at him gratefully. "Time to go."

But when she finally got to bed, she couldn't fall asleep. Instead she lay awake pondering what Niccolo had said, wondering if money and prestige really were strong enough motives for murder.

Friday, Day Four

Chapter 30

Rocky didn't sleep well that night either. Nicco being taken off the case was unwelcome news. As long as his cousin was on it, Rocky had felt confident that Hamish's killer would be found. But now, who knew how long it would take to find the killer? Besides, Nicco had made it clear – it was now up to Rocky.

The faces of the three men he'd seen with Hamish immediately prior to his death flashed through his mind on a loop: Alessandro Fanucci, the slick dealer who had carved a niche for himself as the resident expert in a city built on the history of violins, a man with a lot to lose; Maestro Passero, the respected master violin maker; and Comissario Grassi, the bulldog police chief with friends in high places.

Then there was Fanucci's friend, Massimo Cassiglio, the shady developer who Nicco had intimated managed to straddle both sides of the law. Rocky respected Nicco's intuition and made a mental note to ask him if any of those men were officially considered suspects. He couldn't see what Passero's motive would be, but he had waylaid Hamish outside the restaurant that night, which under the circumstances seemed suspicious. Mia seemed to have

Passero's ear. There might be a way to uncover something there.

Finally, as dawn crept in through his shuttered windows, he got out of bed, grabbed his gear, and hit the streets to catch the sunlight at its soft, golden best. Taking photographs always quieted his left-brain chatter and while his right brain composed pictures with light, he often came out of this photographer's meditation with the answers to at least some of the questions rattling around in his brain.

By eight o'clock he felt somewhat refreshed and met Bernadette as planned at the hotel for a quick breakfast. By nine o'clock they were walking down a road carved into the walls of a dusty hole in the ground that until recently had been a Cremonese town square. Marconi Square, to be exact, a popular shopping area for locals in the heart of the old city. The street layout around the site was typical of the squares in the downtown core: three blocks of shops, with the fourth side the treed edge of a park.

Rocky had noticed the excavation when previously visiting Cremona. He'd been searching the shops around the square for a phone cable and had written the work off as a construction site intended to create a much-needed underground parking lot beneath the square. And it had been, at one time, before they discovered the ruins of the Roman city buried beneath the cobblestones. The possibility of stumbling on remnants of ancient ruins was a potential problem in any Italian construction site. Then *bam*, all work grinds to a halt.

"Archaeologists have known for centuries that there was a Roman town somewhere in the vicinity," Bernadette told him. "And they've known about the battle that took place here. Remnants of the Via Postumia, the Roman road that ran from Genoa to the Adriatic, have been found right here in Cremona during previous excavations. It makes perfect sense. This was the point where a Roman road crossed the Po, so it's not surprising that settlements have grown up on this spot for millennia."

Rocky surveyed the dusty site. It had little to show, compared to other ruins he'd seen in Cambodia and Greece and last year in the Yucatan. "Doesn't look like they've found much."

He turned back to Bernadette to find her sitting on a block of stone, elbows on her knees and her head in her hand.

"Are you okay?"

She looked up and nodded, but her skin tone was ashen. He pushed her head between her knees. She was limp as a piece of cooked linguine. "You're not going to pass out, are you?"

She shook her head, then sat up. "Just chills."

Rocky frowned. He wished he knew exactly what set her off.

She wrapped her arms around her ribs. "It's just the creepy chills I always feel in cemeteries. The history of this place is very dark. I'll be okay in a minute."

Rocky got her water bottle out of her bag and handed it to her. As she drank, he saw her gaze fix on a man across the dig. Hastily, she put the top on her water bottle and waved.

He was tall, and good looking, Rocky noted, sauntering across the dusty dig site, talking to workers as he passed as if he owned the place. He gave Rocky a curious though not unfriendly glance before pulling Bernadette to her feet and wrapping her in a warm embrace.

"Bernadette," he said with heavy Italian emphasis, making the name sound like a familiar pet name. "How you've grown up!"

Bernadette returned the hug warmly, obviously not minding the coating of dust on his clothing. When they broke apart, she said, "Giovanni, I wasn't sure you would remember me."

"Of course I remember Professor Mallow's charming daughter. How could I forget?"

Rocky barely refrained from rolling his eyes.

"But now you are a writer! I thought you would be an archeologist. You were so keen."

"I did study archeology, but now, well, I have a son. I had to settle down."

He nodded. "Yes, is a problem for some women." He turned to Rocky and held out a hand. "But forgive me. Giovanni Presutti, an old friend of Bernadette and her father."

"I'm sorry," Bernadette exclaimed, as if only then remembering that Rocky was there. "This is Rocky Falconi, my partner and photographer."

"A photographer," Giovanni said with enthusiasm. "You must take some photographs of our dig!"

"Sure," Rocky said. Although looking around he thought he'd be hard pressed to find anything worth photographing.

"Have you made any significant discoveries?" Bernadette asked.

"But of course! We have found proof that this is the site of that gruesome battle in 200 B.C., where against all odds, a much smaller Roman army defeated thirty-five thousand Gallic soldiers. It was written in the records one hundred years later, but until we found this site a few years ago, no one knew exactly where the battle took place. That makes this site tremendously important."

Rocky didn't think it sounded so tremendously important, but Bernadette was clearly transfixed by Giovanni's story. She wrapped her arms around her ribs again, as if holding in her excitement. "I thought I felt something when we arrived."

Giovanni put a big hand on her shoulder. "You always were sensitive to spirits."

Bernadette blushed.

Rocky shook his head and looked away. *Seriously?*

Giovanni took them on a tour of the site, which Bernadette obviously found fascinating. The ancient village and everything in it had been destroyed in the battle so, to be polite, Rocky took a number of photographs, he doubted any of them would be interesting enough to use in the article. But there was always a chance of another article. Using information and photographs taken on their Mexican trip, Bernadette found them another job, an article in *Archeology* magazine, and if this was as interesting a find as they seemed to think, he wanted to be prepared in case she managed to line something up with that magazine.

"What else have you planned to see in Cremona?" Giovanni asked.

"We are primarily here for the music festivals," Bernadette said. "But of course I don't want to miss the Archeological Museum."

"Then you must allow me to accompany you!" Giovanni said.

"I'd love that," Bernadette replied enthusiastically. Rocky, it appeared, was not to be consulted. And he had to admit, Giovanni would be a much more interesting and engaged companion on that outing.

"You too, of course," Giovanni said generously to Rocky.

He smiled thinly. "I should get some photographs there too," he acknowledged, but no way did he plan to stay for the tour.

Chapter 31

Two hours later, as they took the freight elevator up to street level from the dig, Rocky said, "Well *that* was interesting."

"I know," Bernadette said enthusiastically, oblivious to his sarcasm. He hoped her excitement was because of the dig – she always got a charge out of dusty holes in the ground – not from the meeting with her old friend.

"Did you know Giovanni was working here?"

A blush crept up to her cheeks. "I did see that in my research before the trip. Of course, I didn't think he'd remember me."

He couldn't stop himself from asking, "Were you good friends?" What he really wanted to know was – *how good?* He shouldn't care about a flame from God only knows how many years ago, who was old enough to be her *father*, but he did.

"Not really," Bernadette said. "I was very young, but I had quite a crush on him." Her features melted in a soft smile. He felt his harden like plaster.

"Wasn't the dig amazing?" she gushed.

"I didn't think there was much to see."

"No, nothing spectacular like the mosaic at Pompeii, but it's the *feel* of the place, the history of the people who lived, and in this case, *died* there." She gave a little shudder as if to shake off the hand of the Reaper. "I couldn't work there, though. The atmosphere of death is too heavy."

Even though Rocky had heard the story Giovanni told and understood the historical importance of the site, he shrugged and said, "I never feel the weight of history the way you do. That's your gift."

She sighed. "Whether I want it or not."

"Let's grab some lunch before we go back to Mondo Musica," Rocky said, turning the conversation away from old flames and ancient death and back to business. "No telling what the food will be like there."

They chose a table in a warm sunny corner of an out-door café near the Duomo Piazza and finished off two caprese salads and a half a bottle of red wine in silence.

Finally Bernadette asked, "What's on your mind?"

He shot her a look, then blew out a breath. "I don't think the police are making any progress in finding Hamish's killer."

Bernadette raised her eyebrows. "So, what are we going to do about it?"

Rocky looked at her in surprise, then smiled. She wasn't going to fight him on beginning his own investigation. "I'm not sure. There is so much going on here this week, it's hard to sort out the strands. Most of it probably has nothing to do with Hamish's death."

"But some of it probably does."

"Yes."

"Well," Bernadette asked, all business. "What do we know?"

"Not much," Rocky admitted. "We know Hamish was here on a story, and it was serious enough that he felt he had to go undercover to hide his identity."

"Because he couldn't get the story if they knew he was a reporter."

"Or he'd be in danger if they found out."

"Which must be what happened."

They stopped for a moment, each lost in their own train of thought, then Bernadette said, "What could be that serious, that dangerous, that they'd kill him when they found out he was a reporter? And who are 'they,' anyway?"

"Exactly. Who? I don't know, but as for the why, there are all the regular offenders; drugs, politics, corruption, crime."

Bernadette swept out her hand to take in the charming, sixteenth century buildings across the street. "Here?"

"Yes. The buildings might be old and charming, but we're still in the twenty-first century with all the modern crime and corruption that goes with it. In fact, there has always been crime and corruption, we just paint medieval times with a rosy brush."

Bernadette laughed. "Not that rosy. I studied life in the Middle Ages in university and I wouldn't trade our life for that flea ridden time for anything."

"And we have to remember this is Italy, where political corruption and underworld crime were invented."

Bernadette sighed. "I guess you're right."

"So all we actually know is that Hamish was on a case," Rocky continued. "He stumbled on something, or dug it out. That was his specialty. Getting a whiff of something underhanded and going after it, nose to the ground, like a hound on a trail. In the past few years it was white collar crime: securities fraud, embezzlement, corporate fraud. Investors don't like it when members of the board abscond with their money. But in this case, it was something worth killing for, but I don't know exactly what that means. Passions run high in Italy."

"Couldn't we contact someone at his paper?" Bernadette asked. "Whoever he was writing the article for?"

Rocky shook his head. "Not an option. He worked on spec. It allowed him the freedom to follow whatever story caught his fancy. And that way, if his hunches panned out, he could sell the article to the highest bidder."

"Hmm," Bernadette mused. "The men we met at the farm said Hamish was going around to violin shops. Do you think that was for the story, or did he really play? Maybe it was just a personal interest."

Rocky thought about that for a minute, then said, "I don't think he played. He never showed any interest in music when we were together. If he was here this week, the story probably had to do with the violin business. I can't imagine what the story could be, though. Except, as we've heard, violins can be worth millions of dollars."

"Money and prestige," Bernadette said, remembering Niccolo's words. "That would be motive for murder. Maybe he uncovered a theft."

"Or a planned theft," Rocky said.

"A ring of thieves," Bernadette added, as possibilities opened before her. "In one of the shops?"

Rocky mulled this over. "We should find out where the high value instruments in the city are this week. Fanucci's booth would be a good place to start. Or maybe Mia knows. But first things first. I want to stop at the hotel before we go back to Mondo Musica."

Chapter 32

"*Grazie,*" Rocky said as the desk clerk handed him his room key.

"*Piacere,*" the clerk responded. The phone rang and he turned away to answer. "*Pronto.*"

On the wall behind the front desk, room keys hung in orderly rows on a board with the room numbers written above them. At this time of day, the board was randomly hung with keys as people returned their keys when they left for the Fiera and other events in town. A heavy brass key hung on a hook marked 301. Hamish's room.

Rocky looked at Bernadette, raised his eyebrows and cocked his head toward the other end of the counter.

She shot a glance at the key rack, then back to him.

"Are you going to help?" he whispered.

"Okay," she said, clutching her key. Then she whispered back, "What should I say?"

He looked at the ceiling in exasperation.

"Okay, okay," she said softly, then walked to the other end of the reception counter. Catching the clerk's eye, she smiled, keeping eye contact with him as she waited for him to finish his call. When he finished, he gave her a gleaming smile and walked further down the counter toward her – away from where Rocky had positioned himself at the other end, near the key rack, where he was leafing through a stack of brochures. "*Si, Signora*, may I help you?"

Rocky got right to work.

"I'm expecting a call, from Canada," Bernadette said. "Will it come straight to my room?"

"No, *Signora*."

Bernadette kept the smile steadily on her face and maintained eye contact with the clerk while he explained how the in-house phone system worked for long distance calls.

Meanwhile, Rocky leaned over the counter and slipped Hamish's key off the peg.

A moment later he was at her side. He smiled at the clerk then said to Bernadette. "Did you get the information you needed?"

"Yes I did." Bernadette smiled at the clerk. "*Grazie*." Then followed Rocky toward the elevator.

Once inside, Bernadette tapped the rail with excitement.

"Maybe you should go back and wait in your room," Rocky said.

"Not a chance," she shot back as the elevator doors opened.

Although it was sunny outside, the windowless hallway was dark. Rocky found the switch on the wall next to the elevator and the hall flashed into brightness.

They hurried down the corridor to Room 301. There was nothing there to indicate it was part of a crime scene. No guard or police tape. As Rocky gave two sharp raps on the door, Bernadette glanced over her shoulder to make sure the hallway was still empty. He put the chunky key in the lock and turned. The click of the lock sounded dangerously loud in the empty corridor.

He wrapped his hand in a handkerchief and reached for the knob. Then, in case the room wasn't empty, called out, "*Pulizia.*" Housekeeping.

The door swung open. The room appeared to be empty. Seconds later another door opened down the hall and youthful voices echoed down the corridor.

Bernadette sucked in a gasp and grabbed Rocky's arm. He swung her into Hamish's room and closed the door.

They stood in silence for a moment in the dim, empty hotel room, their breathing sounding unnaturally loud. The voices grew fainter. Finally the elevator dinged, doors closed and the hall became silent again.

Bernadette rubbed both her hands up and down her arms.

Rocky shot her a glance. "You okay?"

She nodded, but her cheeks were pale and her eyes were unnaturally wide.

Rocky knew that the room had been searched by the police. Niccolo had been part of that. But, he thought, they didn't know Hamish. Didn't know what they were looking for.

Unfortunately, neither did he.

His eyes played over the surfaces of the room. Hamish was a messy guy, and he'd been living in the room for almost a week before he'd been killed. Rocky picked up a pencil and used it to poke through the rubbish on the dresser.

A pile of restaurant receipts, many for the bar at the Continental Hotel. A used hanky rolled up in a ball. Rocky took another pencil and, using them like chopsticks, pulled the handkerchief apart, but there was nothing wrapped inside.

A string of four unused condoms. Black hair dye. Hamish had always taken his undercover work seriously and had seemed to enjoy the costuming aspect.

An open suitcase on the bed, full of what looked like dirty laundry.

Rocky glanced at Bernadette. She stood in the middle of the room, hands trapped under her crossed arms, a faraway look in her eyes. She felt the presence of the dead unlike anyone else he knew, and he wondered what she was feeling now. Her eyes were focused on the closet where one of the louvered doors was ajar.

Rocky walked over to the closet and opened the other door. Pants and shirts and two sports coats hung inside. He systematically checked the pockets of each article of clothing, one by one. Bernadette had followed him to the closet and he could feel breathing lightly behind him, watching over his shoulder. The police had been thorough. The pockets were empty. He knelt, turned over the loafers on the closet floor and tapped. Nothing fell out.

The bathroom only took a few moments to search, even though Rocky took the time to take the tank top off the toilet and check inside.

Back in the bedroom, he stood in the center of the room and looked around. It would help if he knew what he was looking for. He pulled out the desk and dresser drawers, checking the bottoms, hoping to find something taped there, but he was disappointed.

He was out of ideas and moving to the door when he noticed Bernadette still standing by the closet.

"You got anything?" he asked.

She hesitated, then gently ran her hands over each of the shirts hanging on the rod, moving down the row, over the linen sports jacket, then hovered over the tweed.

"This one," she said.

Rocky crossed the room in two long steps. "What is it?"

She shook her head and stepped back, as if touching the clothing was all she could manage.

Rocky took the jacket off the hanger and turned the pockets inside and out. Still empty. He glanced at Bernadette, but her eyes were fixed on the garment in his hands, so he patted down the arms and the seams. Finally, in the lower hem, something crinkled, a piece of paper, trapped inside the lining.

He glanced at Bernadette. She nodded.

He worked his fingers along the lower hem until he found a small, neat rip in the seam. It took a minute or two, working from the outside, to ease the paper back through the interior of the jacket. He widened the rip to fit two fingers and pulled the folded paper out.

It looked like a page torn from a small notebook, then folded into a rectangle the size of a business card. Rocky unfolded it and saw a list of five names, written in pen. An ache of nostalgia flashed through him as he recognized the handwriting.

He flicked the paper with his thumb in satisfaction. "Hamish always liked to play the spy."

Bernadette gave him a quick smile. Back to her old self, she glanced around the room. "I think that's all. Let's get out of here."

Rocky nodded, wrapped his hand in the handkerchief again and slowly opened the door. He looked cautiously into the hall and, seeing it was empty and dark, stepped out of the room with Bernadette close behind. He closed the door and locked it behind them.

Instead of heading for the pale green elevator light, without consultation they turned in the other direction, to the red lit *Uscita* exit sign, at the end of the hall, and walked down one flight of stairs to their rooms.

Once safely inside Rocky's room, Bernadette giggled and rolled her shoulders. "That was fun."

Rocky looked at her in surprise. "Breaking and entering? I would never have pegged you as a cat burglar."

She shook her head and grinned. "Only with you, partner. You bring out the worst in me."

Rocky's room was basic, a mirror image of her own; a double bed, an upholstered side chair with wooden arms, an unmemorable three-drawer dresser that doubled as a nightstand, and a very small desk and chair. Rocky laid the piece of paper on the desk beside his laptop and took the chair.

Bernadette pulled the second chair over beside him and took out her notebook.

"Let's see what we've got," Rocky said as he typed the first name, Gretta Weber, into the browser.

A link to her Facebook page was at the top of the search. Her profile pic showed a young woman, possibly twenty, playing a violin. Apparently she was a grad student at a

German conservatory and played as the soloist with minor local orchestras. Reviews said she was an up and comer. So far, nothing was out of the ordinary. Nothing Rocky could see that would interest Hamish, but Bernadette copied the pertinent information into her notebook anyway.

He moved on to the next name. Jackie Low was a viola player in the Birmingham Symphony as well as a professor at the Royal Birmingham Conservatoire. A high profile local musician but again, nothing unusual.

The third name made Bernadette's breath hitch. Gustaf Braun. Even though they knew him, they ran his name through a google search. It brought up what they expected. A Munich dealer with a polished website, glowing reviews by international musicians, some of whom Bernadette had heard of, expensive instruments for sale and a page about his authentication services.

Other search results linked to papers Braun had written about famous instruments and concerts, and articles others had written about him.

"Pretty well what we knew," Bernadette said.

"I'd bet his meeting with Hamish wasn't coincidental," Rocky added. "I wonder what they talked about."

He typed Jeremy Reynolds, the next name on the list, into the search bar.

"Okay," Rocky said, reading through the results. "He's a violinist with the London Philharmonic Orchestra."

"Wow," Bernadette said, impressed by his list of concert dates. "That name sounds familiar. I don't know where I could have heard it, though. I'm not a real classical music buff."

The last name, scribbled in pencil at the bottom, was possibly the most interesting of all.

"Jay Takeuchi," Bernadette read aloud. "What could he possibly be doing on this list?" She peered at it more closely, holding it under the light. "It seems to have been added later."

They sat in silence for a few minutes, then Rocky said, "What do these people have in common, besides violins, because here this week an interest in violins is pretty well a given."

Bernadette shook her head, and glanced at her notes. "One violin dealer and four violinists who seemed to have studied and now play in four different cities. No two are the same age, or at the same stage of their career. Jay is still in school in the US. Gretta is a German grad student, a few years older than Jay, just starting out in her career. Jeremy Reynolds is older, a violinist with the London Philharmonic Orchestra. And didn't it say the fourth one – "

"Jackie Lowe," Rocky supplied.

"Jackie Lowe," Bernadette repeated, "isn't a violin player at all. Didn't she play the viola?"

"And Gustaf is a dealer."

"Two Brits, Two Germans and one American," Bernadette said, trying the data another way and still coming up with nothing.

They sat in silence for a few minutes mulling over the new information, then Rocky stood up and slipped on his jacket. "Let's go rattle a few chains."

Chapter 33

M ondo Musica was in full swing when they got there. The shuttle bus had been packed and the line to enter the arena stretched out the door and down the sidewalk. Luckily their passes from Mia, and a smile at the usher from Rocky, got them in quickly.

Once inside, they made their way through the noise and congestion, looking for Gustaf Braun.

As they passed Passero's booth, Mia called out, "Meet at the shop tonight?"

They agreed to meet her there at eight for a tour, then go out for dinner.

Gustaf Braun was in his booth, busy talking to clients. His assistant approached them, asking if he could be of help, but they told him they preferred to wait. Twenty minutes later, Gustaf was finally free and approached them with a sheepish smile. "I am sorry my friends, but it has been very busy today. Which is a good thing. How can I help you?"

"May we have a minute of your time?" Bernadette asked.

"Certainly. It is time for a break. Let us escape and find an espresso."

Huddled around a standup table in the crowded coffee bar a few minutes later, Bernadette got right to the point. "We found a list of people and wondered if you know any of them, or what they have in common."

Gustaf, looking downright professorial in his half-glass-es glasses and tweed jacket, read the list. "What? *I* am on this list. What is this list?"

Bernadette glanced at Rocky to make sure it was all right to share this information. He gave a slight nod, so she said, "It was Amos Ballantyne's. Do you know what these people have in common?"

"I know a few of these people. Or know of them. Gretta Webber I do know. She is a promising young violinist from Ingolstadt, an hour by car from Munich. She has been to my shop several times." He frowned. "I said the same to Amos. I don't know where he got her name." He shook his head and referred to the list. "And I have also heard of Jeremy Reynolds, British, but I do not know him person-ally. My friend Matty Dean might know him. Matty used to work at Hill's violin shop in London. Now he works for Sotheby's, appraising violins. He knows everyone. He might be at the Sotheby's booth now.

"And of course Jay Takeuchi is a Crown contestant." Gustaf shook his head and handed back the list. "That is all I know. Sorry not to be of more help. Is it important?"

"It might be,' Rocky said, putting the piece of paper back in his pocket. "Do me a favor. Be careful."

Gustaf puffed out his cheeks. "I don't think I am in any danger, but as you advise, I will be careful. Now I must get back. This weekend is like gold and any minutes I am not in my booth are possible coins slipping through my fingers. Maybe we can talk again. At Castello Maria perhaps?"

"Yes. I'd like that," Bernadette said, scribbling the name 'Matty Dean' in her notebook. "And thank you for your time."

As Gustaf disappeared into the crowd, she closed her book with a satisfied thump. "Where to now? Sotheby's?"

Rocky nodded, tossed his tiny paper cup into the trash and stalked away, Bernadette following him into the fray.

Sotheby's booth was two rows over at the far end of the arena. Unlike other booths, it was not lined with violins. Instead, it was tastefully decorated with a desk and chairs at one end and a settee and upholstered chair at the other. As an auction house, Bernadette figured they were more interested in lining up consignments than making sales this weekend.

They asked for Matty Dean and were directed to a nattily dressed man of around fifty years of age who was sitting at the desk. Rocky slid into what Bernadette thought of as his grease-the-wheels charmer mode. After exchanging greetings and explaining that their "good friend" Gustaf Braun suggested they speak to him, Natty warmed up considerably.

"We are looking for some people who spoke to our friend Amos Ballantyne during the week before he died," Rocky said.

"I heard about that," Matty said, nodding. Then he looked at the floor and shook his head. "Nasty business. Word is, it was murder."

"Did you meet him?" Bernadette asked. She sensed he was eager to spread what he'd heard.

"No, I didn't. Although he'd only been here for a few days, he seems to have really done the rounds. A lot of the fellows seem to have met him."

"Which fellows?" Rocky asked.

"Well, Alessandro Fanucci for one."

"Yes, we've spoken to him," Rocky said. "We're looking for another man we heard he'd been talking to, a Jeremy Reynolds. Gustaf said you might know him."

Matty nodded and scanned the crowd as if Jeremy might be out there somewhere in the throng. "Yes, I've seen him around. He's interested in selling a violin at our spring auction. I hope it's not the one he showed me last year. I couldn't authenticate that one for the sale."

"Why not?" Bernadette asked.

"It was a fake. Had papers, but in my opinion it wasn't a Ruggiere. And I have to go with my gut, for the sake of the firm. Sotheby's has a reputation to protect."

"I understand," Rocky said. "Have you seen Jeremy today?"

"Not today. He might have already left Cremona. He looked pretty shaken yesterday."

"What about?" Rocky asked. "Did he say?"

"Not really. He was talking about Ballantyne though. Apparently Amos had been to see him the afternoon before he was killed. Jeremy seemed worried, but wouldn't admit it, and he wouldn't say what he was worried about."

"You wouldn't happen to know where he was staying would you?" Bernadette asked.

"Most of the Brits are holed up at The Continental. If you are around tonight I'll meet you there for a drink at ten, after the Fiera closes," Matty said.

Rocky nodded. "Sounds like a plan."

The air was hot and humid in the overcrowded shuttle bus as it crept back into town through the late afternoon traffic. Even Cremona had a rush hour, Bernadette supposed. The bus was packed with tired but happy tradeshow-goers, chatting about the gorgeous instruments they'd seen and played. Bernadette and Rocky weren't lucky enough to get seats so it was a tiring half hour of jostling with strangers as the bus wound its circuitous route over the cobblestone streets of the town and out the other side.

They disembarked at the Continental Hotel, a large, featureless, white stucco structure with a sweeping drive on the edge of town. Her own room at the Hotel Cremona might border on generic, but Bernadette was glad they were staying in the charming heart of the old town instead of here on the edge of the city.

The young woman clerk behind the reception desk was stiff and formal at first but soon succumbed to Rocky's charm. She flirtatiously flipped her hair back over her shoulder as she gave him Jeremy Reynolds' room number. When he turned back to Bernadette, he was all business again and she wondered, just for a second, why he so rarely turned that smile on her.

"We're supposed to phone up first," he said, nodding and smiling back at the clerk, then heading for a bank of house phones on the wall nearby. He punched in a number and after a few seconds said, "Hi. It's me."

Bernadette frowned. How could Jeremy Reynolds know who "me" was?

"Sure, we'll be right up," Rocky said, and hung up the phone.

"Come on," he said to Bernadette and headed for the elevator.

"Was he home?" Bernadette asked in a low voice, glancing at the receptionist who was busy on the computer.

"Didn't answer. But let's go up anyway. Just to see."

The Continental was tired and rundown. The fourth floor corridor smelled of stale room service food and the lighting was dim. Rocky stopped at room four ten and knocked. No one answered, so he and Bernadette both put their ears to the door, nodding to each other when they heard noises inside. Someone was there.

Bernadette raised her eyebrows, silently asking, *what now*? Rocky knocked again, this time with more authority.

A moment later the door opened a crack, and a man peered out. "Who are you?" he asked timidly.

"Friends of Amos Ballantyne," Rocky said.

Jeremy's eyes widened. Bernadette feared he'd close the door in their faces, so she added quickly, "Matty Dean sent us."

The door closed and the chain rattled as it slid off the lock. Jeremy opened the door, glancing furtively up and down the hall as he motioned them inside, immediately closing and locking the door behind them. Bernadette could see he was scared, probably of whoever had killed Hamish. But why would he think they would come after him?

"What did Matty tell you?" Jeremy asked abruptly. No, *please sit down* or, *would you like something to drink?* This was obviously not going to be a social call.

"Matty didn't tell us anything," Rocky said.

"Then why are you here?"

"We found your name on a list in Amos Ballantyne's room and tracked you down."

Jeremy's eyes widened in alarm. He ran a hand through his shock of red hair, not, by the look of it, for the first time. His shirt was untucked and he was barefoot. The curtains were drawn and takeout food containers littered the dresser and night table. He looked like he was hiding out. Then Bernadette noticed the full, open suitcase on the unmade bed and changed her mind. Not hiding out; he looked like a man on the run.

"What kind of list?" he asked.

"A list of names. We don't know how or even if it is connected to Amos's death. We don't know what story he was working on. That's what we are trying to find out," Rocky said.

"You knew him?"

"He was my friend. His real name was Hamish Gladstone."

Jeremy blew out a breath and relaxed for the first time. "That was the name I knew him by when I first met him in London."

Bernadette and Rocky glanced at each other. So, Hamish had known Jeremy before this trip. This could finally be their first solid lead.

"In fact," he said, and Bernadette was horrified to see tears well up in his eyes. He sat down abruptly on a chair and dropped his head into his hand. "I am the one who got him killed."

Chapter 34

Rocky pulled up the only other chair in the room close to Jeremy and sat. "What do you mean?"

Jeremy leaned back, suddenly eager to tell his story. "We met at a party in London after a concert. I'm with the London Philharmonic. Hamish said he was a journalist and, well, I was pissed off at the time because I felt like I'd been ripped off, swindled out of all my savings, so I said to him, 'I'll tell you a story.' And I did. I had no idea he'd come to Cremona, and, well..."

He obviously couldn't finish the sentence, so Bernadette said encouragingly, "Of course you didn't."

"What was the story?" Rocky asked.

"Five years ago I was here at Mondo Musica. I had just got the gig with the Philharmonic and I was stoked. At the time I had a good violin, a Morassi, but I decided to invest in something better. Something really good. You know?"

Rocky and Bernadette both nodded. It was virtually the same story they'd heard from Jay.

"So I came a few days early and asked around. One of the local shops recommended I talk to Fanucci. Actually, everyone I spoke to said he was the one who would know what was available. So I did, I asked him and he said he knew a private collector who wanted to sell an old violin, a Ruggiere, which he thought was a good deal. Fanucci said he'd manage the deal, take my violin in trade and give me papers of authenticity for the new violin. It took all my savings but I was feeling good about the new job. It paid more money than I'd been making before and I thought it was time to step up.

"Everything went smoothly during the deal. I loved the violin, still play it, but after I'd had it for a year I took it to Hill's to get new strings on it."

Bernadette nodded. "And what did they say?"

"They said it was nice, probably Italian, probably two hundred years old, but in their opinion, not a Ruggiere. They suggested I get a second opinion from Matty Dean. He didn't think it was a real one either. Old, yes, but not that old, and unless I wanted to send it to a dendrochronology lab – which is terribly expensive – there was no way of proving differently."

"So what did you do?" Rocky prompted.

Jeremy's shoulders slumped again. "What could I do? The violin came with Fanucci papers. Who was I to argue with him?" He shook his head. "I was a chump. I should have been smarter. I should have had someone else look at it before I bought it." He shrugged, resigned. "It happens."

"So we've been hearing," Bernadette said.

"And you told all this to Hamish?" Rocky asked.

"I did. I had no idea he'd go after Fanucci." His voice rose. "I had no idea it would get him killed. We met a couple of times last week, and I'm afraid whoever killed Hamish saw us together and now they'll come after me!"

"Did you know he was going to be here this week?" Bernadette asked, trying to keep the conversation on track.

Jeremy nodded. "He called me about a month ago. Said he'd been doing a little digging and it seemed as if I wasn't the only one who'd been scammed by Fanucci. I was kind of excited, wanted to see the guy brought down, you know? So I said sure, I'd come back this year and confront Fanucci. I could have stood to get some of that money back, although I guess that's not going to happen.

"Hamish said it sounded like fun and he would join me here. I didn't realize he would come ahead and try to set up a sting. We met for drinks as soon as I arrived. And again the next day. Then the following day, he was murdered. We never had a chance to go to Fanucci, and there's absolutely no way I'd confront him now. In fact, I'm going to get out of here as quickly as I can. I'll take the train to Brescia tonight and connect with an early flight back to London tomorrow morning."

Rocky nodded. "I understand. One more thing, though. Who was the previous owner of this violin?"

"Massimo Cassiglio."

Bernadette and Rocky shared a glance .Cassiglio. Fanucci's shady friend.

Chapter 35

I t was dusk when they stepped out of The Continental and onto the circular drive, and colder than it had been that afternoon.

"Let's grab a cab," Rocky said. He raised his hand and a moment later a sleek Mercedes pulled up beside them.

As soon as they were in the car, Bernadette said, "So, that was interesting."

Rocky shook his head. "We'll talk about it later."

Bernadette sighed. Right. The cabby. She settled back in the seat for the short ride to their hotel. Cremona was a small city, little more than a town, and Rocky was probably right. Any information about the murder of the mysterious stranger would be prize gossip.

After a quick pit stop in her room to prepare for Passero's shop tour with Mia that evening, Bernadette started back to meet Rocky in the lobby.

Music poured out into the corridor from Tatiana's room, and Bernadette paused to listen. It was a piece she remembered playing, one of Bartok's Romanian Folk Dances, but she had never played it this well. The melody tugged at her heart strings. Peeking through the partially open door, she saw Tatiana, swaying to the music as she wove an irresistible spell.

With a loud twang, the music suddenly stopped. There was a moment of total silence, then a flood of what sounded, from the impassioned delivery, like Romanian curses.

Bernadette couldn't stop herself. She stuck her head inside the partially open door. Tatiana was holding her violin by the neck. A string curled from one of the pegs at the top, obviously broken. Mirela was standing there too, trying to talk Tatiana down.

Mirela saw Bernadette, sent her a commiserating smile, as if to say, *musicians, so temperamental*, and switched to English. "It is just a string. I will get it fixed." She wrestled the instrument from Tatiana's reluctant hands.

"But the second concert is tomorrow!"

"I will get it back in plenty of time."

"But how will I practice? I can not win if I don't practice."

"I will have it back right after breakfast. You can warm up tomorrow morning. That will be all you need. You know the piece front and back."

The girl looked bereft as Mirela locked the violin in its case and swept out of the room, looking strangely triumphant, like she'd won – something. Bernadette wasn't sure exactly what.

As Mirela exited, Tatiana made a small sound, like a whimpering puppy.

Bernadette stepped into the room, and Tatiana finally registered her presence with a start. Bernadette took another step toward her and said in her most comforting, motherly voice, "It will be okay. I'm sure in this town

Mirela will have no trouble finding someone very good to fix it."

The girl didn't reply, just looked longingly at the door her violin had recently passed through. Bernadette took her hands and gently pulled her down until they both sat on the edge of the bed.

"I have to win this competition," Tatiana said in a low, determined voice. She looked Bernadette in the eye. "I *have* to win. My mother is sick. She needs medicine we cannot afford. I *need* the money." Her shoulders slumped. "I have to win."

Bernadette's heart went out to the girl. No wonder she was so somber and driven, with the burden of her mother's health – possibly her mother's life – hanging over her head.

Now that there was a crack in the dam, the whole story burst out. "I am the only one who can help her. We have no other family. We are from a small town in the northern Romania. Transylvanian. It is not like here. If you are sick, you must go to the city, and then you must find a doctor who is willing to treat you. Half the time, even if the doctor will look at you, there are no drugs. My mother is diabetic, her feet are infected. If she does not get treatment soon, she could die." The girl sobbed again.

"You are an excellent violinist," Bernadette said staunchly. Finding a fresh tissue in her purse, she handed it to Tatiana. "I think you are the best in the competition. There is a very good chance you will win."

Tatiana sniffed and used the tissue to wipe her eyes. "But you are not a judge. Sometimes not the best player wins."

There was little Bernadette could say to that. It was sad but probably true. She knew politicking went on behind the scenes at many competitions and the most deserving player might not always win in the end.

"Well," she said heartily, pulling Tatiana to her feet. "You'll get your violin back after breakfast and the competition is not until the afternoon. There will be time to warm up before you have to play. For now, please don't worry. Come downstairs and we'll have dinner. Together."

"I was supposed to have dinner with some of the other contestants," Tatiana said tentatively.

"Great," Bernadette said, suddenly remembering that she and Rocky had arranged to meet Mia for dinner. "I'm going to go." She squatted slightly to look the girl in the eye. "Are you going to be all right?"

Tatiana smiled bravely, if somewhat tearily. "I will be fine. And thank you."

Chapter 36

Bernadette met Rocky in the lobby. It was dusk when they stepped out onto the narrow, cobblestone street and a faint haze drifted overhead, creating halos around the amber lights that dotted the dark road.

They walked through Piazza Duomo, then along Via Solferino toward the central park, Piazza Roma. At this hour, the street was humming with activity, mostly people shopping on their way home from work, in and out of the open stores that beamed warm light onto the cobblestone street.

"They stay open late," Bernadette observed.

"Most of them were closed for a few hours in the afternoon," Rocky said.

"Still?" Bernadette had experienced *la pausa*, an old custom like the Spanish *siesta*, when she'd been at the dig in southern Italy with her father years ago, but she was surprised to find it still practiced in such a modern city. "Sounds bad for business."

Rocky shrugged. "Sounds civilized to me. Everyone goes home and relaxes, has a good meal, maybe a nap, then comes back, refreshed."

Most of the storefronts were ultra-modern, doing their best to deny the age of the building that housed them by displaying the latest styles in clothing and home furnishings from Milan. But one stood out from the lot. Like it belonged to a bygone era, the words '*torrone* and *mostarda*' were painted above on windows in elaborate gold script. The glass door opened and a group of people came out onto the street, smiling and clutching their bags of treasure, the sweet smell of sugar wafting out after them.

"Maybe your son would like a box of Torrone candy," Rocky suggested, indicating a display of white boxes in the window. "Cremona is famous for it."

Bernadette's face lit up. "Good idea. What is it made from?"

"It's nougat candy. Usually with almonds," Rocky said, steering her over to the tower of boxes on display in the window.

"And *mostarda*? Mustard?"

"Mmm, not really. It's a traditional condiment with mustard in it, but preferably oil of mustard, wine, and lots of chunks of fruit that end up candied. A bit sweet, a bit spicy. Hard to explain. A local specialty," Rocky said, holding the door open for her to enter. "Come on. We have time. Let's try it."

Inside, wooden counters were piled high with bright boxes of candy, and bins of individually wrapped treats stood on the worn wooden floor. Half an hour later, Rocky again held the door open for Bernadette, this time so she could exit with her arms full of bags.

"Are they all gifts?" he asked.

She laughed self-consciously. "Not all. I'll keep some for myself. But I like to take presents back for Colin and my mother. Mom will love that dessert wine."

Rocky winced.

Bernadette laughed again. "Not your favorite?"

"I like something a little dryer. But your mother might like it."

They passed a small violin maker's shop. The old town was peppered with them. The maker's name was worked into a modern design on the frosted window.

"Where is Fanucci's shop" she asked.

"Right beside Passero's."

"Funny, I didn't notice it the other day. Helmut mentioned he'd met Hamish there, right?"

Rocky nodded. "Helmut and Nicco both mentioned Hamish had been there."

"I remember because it was the first time I realized that someone could *forge* a violin," Bernadette said.

"It would take a lot of skill," Rocky acknowledged. "But it would be worth it. If you could get away with it."

"Could you really forge a Stradivarius?" Bernadette asked. It seemed impossible.

Rocky shook his head. "Probably not. Too bold. Maybe a slightly less well-known name. Some of his contemporaries' violins are worth a pretty penny too."

She smirked. "A pretty penny? What century are you from?"

Rocky shrugged one shoulder. "Something my mom always says. She loves English idioms."

"Do your parents speak Italian at home?"

"It depends on what they're talking about. For work, current politics, things like that they speak English. And with us kids. But for talking about the family, day to day things, with each other, they speak Italian."

"No wonder your Italian is so good."

"Nonna, my grandmother, lives with them in San Francisco and she speaks only Italian. What I knew when I arrived here a few years ago was from her. My Cremona cousins teased me, saying I spoke such an archaic form of the language that they could hardly understand me. And you tease me for my archaic English. I can't win." He tried to look hard done by, but Bernadette just laughed.

At Piazza Roma they crossed the road and entered the park where lights strung on the boughs of spreading deciduous trees cast an eerie glow through the shifting leaves. It had felt so different when they'd passed through yesterday morning on their way to meet Paola. Then the park had been full of mothers calling to young children and grannies in black dresses gossiping on park benches.

"I saw men playing bocce ball here yesterday," Bernadette said.

Rocky laughed. "It's "buh-chee," not "bah-chee." In Italian, *baci* means kiss. So *baci* ball, well... it sends the wrong message. The old guys love it."

She snorted. "I bet."

They were silent for a minute and Bernadette sensed Rocky's mind had gone back to Hamish's murder.

"So, Jeremy's an interesting development," she said.

"At first, I couldn't see how the names on the list connected with any of our prime suspects, the men Hamish sat with in the restaurant our first evening here. His last evening. But Jeremy's story connects at least some of them."

"But would Fanucci be so blatant as to murder someone for digging into his business? Surely he could see it would draw too much attention to whatever it is he is doing."

"What he seems to be doing is selling counterfeit violin papers," Rocky said. "Or maybe even counterfeit instruments."

"But is that worth killing for?"

"It might be," Rocky said thoughtfully. "You saw his house. He must have a pretty sweet deal going here to be able to afford that. And I wouldn't want to cross that big guy."

"Cassiglio?"

"Right. I'd bet he and Fanucci are in it together. Whatever it is."

Chapter 37

Passero's shop stood out in the middle of the block of four-hundred-year-old buildings facing the park as the only one that was brightly lit in the darkness. The ground floor shop window, a large, semi-circular window on the second floor, and four smaller windows on the third floor were all aglow.

This time, Bernadette recognized Fanucci's name on the window of the shop beside Passero's. She must have walked right past it the other morning without noticing, her attention waylaid by the lingerie draped artistically over the violin in the window next door. And that was before they had met Fanucci at Mondo Musica. The front window of his shop was frosted, a violin in a circle etched in the middle of the glass. A dim light burned in a back room, but other than that, there was nothing to see.

"Very classy. Looks like a lawyer's office," Bernadette said softly, so as not to be overheard by the heavy-set man leaning against the back of the black four-door Maserati parked at the curb.

Rocky nodded to him. "Ciao."

The man gave them a curt nod and eyed them steadily as they walked past.

"Wonder who that belongs to?" Bernadette asked, under her breath.

Rocky gave a slight shake of his head. "That's a lot of muscle for a chauffeur," he murmured.

Mia burst through the door of Passero's shop, greeting them enthusiastically. "Ciao, ciao," she said, kissing each of them vigorously on both cheeks, giving Rocky a third peck for good measure.

After they'd stepped inside, Rocky inclined his head to the big front window. "Who's the guy with the car."

Mia peeked out and frowned. "That is Fanucci's driver."

Bernadette's eyes widened. "Fanucci must sell a lot of violins to have a driver and a car like that."

Rocky glanced out again. "Niccolo hinted he might be doing more than just selling violins."

"I still find that hard to believe," Bernadette said.

"I know Cremona looks like a gentle, historic city, and the violin overlay gives it a classy sheen, but underneath it's just like any other twenty-first century city. And remember," he said cryptically, pulling out his camera. "This is Italy."

Bernadette looked at him askance. "And what does *that* mean?"

He looked at her as if she were slow. "Organized crime."

"In Cremona?"

"We're not that far from Milan, the biggest drug importing city in Italy," Mia said. "You would think it would come in through organized crime in the south or Rome, but apparently, recently, it's Milan." At Bernadette's astonished expression, Mia just shrugged.

Bernadette wanted more details, but Mia had turned away and was leading them back into the shop. When she started talking again, she had changed the subject. Obviously, organized crime was nothing new in Cremona and nothing Mia was interested in talking about.

"This is our store, where customers come to try out our instruments." She indicated the empty racks on the walls. "Of course, all of the violins are at the show right now."

"Do you only make violins here?" Bernadette asked, pulling out her pad as they walked to the back of the store.

"Not only, just mostly. A few violas, and one of the apprentices is making a cello. Of course, we also do repairs and Maestro Pissarro does authentications as well."

That was interesting. Apparently Fanucci wasn't the only expert on old instruments in town.

The shop was narrow and deep with a high ceiling and empty counters lining the walls. It was all business up front, but in the back they reached a casual seating area.

From there, Mia led them up a long stairway built against an ancient red brick wall, to the huge, second storey workshop that stretched the length of the building. Rocky got right to work, taking pictures from every angle, turning lights on and off to get the look he wanted as Mia spoke to Bernadette.

"This is where everyone works. Well, all of the apprentices."

"Not Passero?" Bernadette asked, eyes on her pad, taking notes.

"No. He has a bench there overlooking the street." Mia pointed to an old workbench that carried the scars of years of work, the deep gouges and scrapes telling the story of the birth of countless instruments. Set up in front of the semi-circular window whose mullions radiated out like the spokes of a wheel, you would have a bird's eye view of intimate life in Piazza Roma, the family heart of the town for hundreds of years.

"But he does not work down here much anymore."

"Where does he work?" Rocky asked.

"He spends a lot of time in his rooms upstairs." Mia pointed to the ceiling.

Now that she mentioned it, Bernadette realized faint sounds were emanating through the ceiling. It wasn't insulated, just the bare boards of the floor above, where she could hear someone walking. She could also hear muffled voices. From the sound of it he, or she, wasn't alone.

"Does he live up there?" she asked, lowering her voice.

"He does now." Mia glanced at the ceiling. "The Maestro used to have another apartment in town but when his wife died, he moved up there. He has another workshop upstairs, too. We hear him there every evening. Actually, we are all dead curious about what he does up there." She laughed. "We joke he's up there watching porn – we know he invites women over sometimes. But really, I have no idea. None of us has ever been invited up."

Bernadette looked at the creaking ceiling high above. He must have invited someone up tonight.

"I guess that's his staircase," she observed, pointing to a narrow set of stairs that ran up one of the brick side walls of the building and through an opening in the ceiling.

"There is a private staircase from the street as well," Mia said, starting back down the stairs to the main floor.

Bernadette thought that must be how whoever was up there now had entered since they hadn't seen anyone in the shop.

Rocky followed them, stopping on a landing halfway down the stairs to get a shot of the store from above. "I'd like to come back in the daylight, both when people are working and when the place is empty. If that's okay."

"We'll all be at Mondo Musica tomorrow, but I could open the door for you before I leave in the morning."

"Terrific. That's when the light will be best. What time?"

"Nine o'clock?"

Upon reaching the ground floor, Mia walked over to the rear conversation area where she pulled a bottle of wine out from under a corner coffee table. "Care for a drink?"

"Sure," Rocky said.

Bernadette glanced at him. She could tell he was trying to look casual, but she could feel the energy radiating off him. This was the perfect opportunity to find out more about Passero, the man Hamish had been speaking to on the street right before he was killed.

Chapter 38

While Mia rounded up the wine glasses, Rocky took a seat on one of the sleek chairs in the informal conversation area at the rear of the shop.

"We often serve wine to our customers," she said. "Sometimes they are here for hours trying instruments and a glass or two helps them decide."

When they were settled, Bernadette asked. "Do you ever sell violins by other makers? Any old violins?"

"We have a few old ones. No other modern makers, though. Passero only sells his own and those of his apprentices. The Maestro is passionate about his apprenticeship program so sometimes he will show an instrument made by one of his apprentices who has gone out on their own. Maestro Passero does not make many violins himself these days."

Her voice dropped to a whisper even though there was no one there to hear. "His eyesight is very poor, not good enough to do much of his own work anymore and he wears thick glasses when he is looking at our work."

She sat back and her voice returned to its normal level. "He keeps a few old violins upstairs in his attic studio and brings them down for special clients. Or, for *very* special clients, he will take them upstairs." She dropped her chin and nodded suggestively.

This wasn't the first time Mia had hinted that Passero liked the ladies.

"I guess that makes sense," Bernadette said. "How often do really old violins come on the market? Like, three-hundred-year-old violins?"

"Once in a while Fanucci will find one and if it needs work he will give it to the Maestro to repair. But he does that up in this private studio."

Rocky perked up. "Have you heard about any surfacing lately? I mean, you read about old Strads being found that were seized by the Nazis or the Communist regimes. Or stolen years ago."

"That's true," Mia said. Her eyes sparkled and she reverently dropped her voice. "I have heard that one surfaced this year. A Guarneri *del Gesù*."

Rocky saw by the way Bernadette straightened in her chair that she too had caught the reference to the maker that Jay had mentioned. The maker of the violin that Jay and Tatiana had played in Fanucci's booth, the one that Jay wanted to buy.

"Have you seen it?" Bernadette asked.

"Only for a few minutes. Fanucci gave it to Maestro Passero to re-string, and he showed it to us all then."

"I guess something that old would need a lot of work," Rocky mused.

Mia shook her head. "You would try to do as little as possible, to preserve the original finish and not disturb the patina. Unless of course something catastrophic had happened, like the stolen Stradivarius that a street musician had painted black and been playing on street corners for years."

"Imagine!" Bernadette exclaimed.

Mia grinned and shrugged one shoulder. "It is a well-known story."

"What about the Guarneri?" Rocky asked, trying to get the discussion back on topic. "Are there many of them still around?"

"Actually, there were four violin makers in the Guarneri family at the time of Stradivari. Giuseppe Guarneri, the grandson, is considered the best maker in the family. Giuseppe's career was short – he only lived forty-six years. Today, his violins rival Strads for favour with musicians. But compared to Stradivari, his workmanship was inconsistent."

"How so?" Rocky asked.

"Strad found something that worked and was almost like a machine, producing very consistent instruments. That makes them relatively easy for experts to identify. Giuseppe Guarneri, however, was always experimenting, trying different shapes of f-holes, arching, thicknesses of the wood. In fact, in his later years, some of his violins were pretty rough and poorly finished."

"I guess they don't sound as good as a Strad," Bernadette suggested.

Mia shook her head. "Not the case! The sound is *magnifico*, even in the later instruments. Some players think they sound better than a Strad. They say that Stradivari was a businessman, but Guarneri was an artist." She shrugged one shoulder toward her chin. "Is an ongoing battle."

Picking up the bottle, she poured them all more wine. "There are legends about Giuseppe, but now experts think he did not make enough money to live on, so he had to work quickly and use materials that were less than ideal. Rumor has it that in his last years he ran an inn and made violins on the side, perhaps with the help of his wife. One legend even says Guarneri made his later instruments in jail! The stories all just feed his mystique, but there is no denying the powerful sound of his violins."

"Are they worth as much as a Strad?" Rocky asked.

"They have close to the same value, partly because they are so rare. There are still so many more Strads."

After a moment, Rocky said thoughtfully, "I suppose over the years the inconsistencies would make the Guarneri's easier to forge."

"Yes, it is true, and forgeries have been discovered."

"That's terrible!" Bernadette exclaimed.

Mia shrugged. "No one works too hard to find the fakes. It's to no one's advantage to have their violin shown to be a forgery."

"Except, perhaps, the buyer," Rocky said thoughtfully. "Before the money changes hands."

"Maybe," Mia agreed. They were all silent for a moment, thinking that over. Then she downed the last of her wine and asked brightly, "Time to eat?"

She quickly tidied away the evidence of their party, then ushered them both to the door. As they stepped out onto the sidewalk, Rocky noticed Jay, Gloria and Fanucci standing in front of Fanucci's shop next door. Rocky exchanged a quick glance with Bernadette and they stepped back into the shadows.

Jay's back was to them, and he was pulling his hand out of his back pocket as if he had just put his wallet away, or perhaps had put something into his pocket. Then, he shook Fanucci's hand, took a violin case from Gloria, and they walked away, back toward the hotel.

Fanucci turned and started slightly when he noticed Rocky and Bernadette standing twenty feet away. He gave them a formal nod of recognition and quickly climbed into the backseat of the car that was still waiting at the curb. The motor was running and the same burly driver was behind the wheel. The car quickly peeled away from the curb.

Mia joined them just as an inset door between the two shops opened and Mirela stepped out onto the sidewalk. She hesitated when she saw the three of them standing so nearby, and Rocky thought for a moment that she might go back inside. But since they had obviously seen her, she too nodded in their direction and took off hurriedly on foot in the direction of the hotel.

"Busy place," Bernadette murmured softly as they watched her go.

Mia nodded. "It is Mondo Musica." She rubbed her thumb and index finger together. "There's money to be made and only a few days to do it."

"Is that the doorway to Passero's flat?" Rocky asked.

Mia nodded, but was obviously not interested in what Mirela was doing in the maestro's flat. Instead, she said, "I know a little place just around the corner that serves a risotto to die for."

Chapter 39

They kept dinner short so that Bernadette and Rocky could meet with Matty Dean again as planned. This time they retrieved the Cinquecento and drove to the Continental Hotel. Unlike the darkened streets the night they arrived, the town was alight, now that Mondo Musica was in full swing. On every corner, restaurant doors were thrown open and happy customers, loud and laughing and feeling their wine, spilled out to tables set up on the narrow sidewalks.

The Cinquecento pulled neatly into a small spot in the packed guest parking lot at the Continental. When they walked into the hotel restaurant, Bernadette spotted Matty Dean at the bar, regaling his fellows with what was obviously an hilarious story. When the punchline had been delivered and appropriately appreciated, Matty's compatriots dispersed. Rocky put on a friendly smile and clapped a hand on Matty's shoulder.

Matty turned clumsily on his swivel seat grabbing the counter for support. "My man, you made it. And your lovely partner too."

Bernadette smiled a greeting, and they took the now-empty stools beside him. Matty had been drinking, probably for a while, but that was okay. It might make it easier to get the information they were looking for.

"Can I buy you a drink?" Rocky asked genially.

Matty winked broadly at Bernadette. "I never say no."

Rocky turned to Bernadette, eyebrows raised in question.

"Campari and soda, please," she said. She wanted to keep her wits about her. Rocky was so intent on solving Hamish's case – not that she blamed him – that she didn't feel he was being discreet. Almost, she would venture to say, a bit reckless. There had, after all, been one murder already.

When their drinks arrived, Rocky steered the conversation to old violins up for auction at Sotheby's in their next instrument sale.

"Nothing really special at the moment," Matty said. "Not yet, anyway. But there's still time," he added hopefully.

"I've been hearing about a newly discovered Guarneri *del Gesù* in town," Rocky said. "At Fanucci's."

Bernadette squinted in thought, remembering how Fanucci had denied having anything that special when they'd talked to him at his booth, yet apparently now he was offering one to Jay. So why would he not have mentioned it to them when they specifically asked about precious old instruments? And, more importantly, had he offered it to Hamish? Surely competition for the instrument would only drive up the price, which in turn would be good for Fanucci. Unless he had a reason to keep it aside for Jay.

Matty shook his head. "Haven't heard anything about that." Then he brightened up in an alcohol induced mood swing. "But where's our friend Jeremy?" He swung around on the bar stool to look around the room, almost ending up on the floor. Bernadette put out a hand to steady him, wondering if he might already be too far gone to be of any use to them tonight.

"I think Jeremy might have left town," Bernadette said.

Matty shook his head loosely. "Nope, I asked at the desk when I got back tonight and he hadn't checked out."

"Must have changed his mind," Rocky murmured, his eyes narrowing.

Matty pulled his cell phone out of his pocket and punched in a number. "I'll give him a ring." After a minute he shook his head. "No answer. That's weird. Where would he have gone without his mobile?"

Bernadette's stomach lurched and she felt the blood drain from her cheeks. She couldn't focus as darkness advanced from both sides of her field of vision. She put a hand on Rocky's arm and said, "We have to go up to his room."

Rocky took one look at Bernadette and knew something was wrong. She'd gone deathly pale and her unblinking eyes were wide. Her Spidey sense was at it again.

"You stay here. I'll go check," he said.

She closed her eyes and shook her head.

"Whatever," Matty muttered, and turned to greet a man who slid into the seat on his other side.

Throwing some Euros on the bar, Rocky headed for the elevator with Bernadette right on his tail. He punched the UP button impatiently, but when the elevator doors slid open, they were face to face with Jeremy Reynolds.

"We called you," Bernadette said, blowing out a relieved breath. "But you didn't answer."

"I thought it was Matty," Jeremy said, struggling out of the elevator with his heavy duffle bag and violin case. He set the duffle bag down on the terrazzo floor.

"It was Matty," Rocky conceded. "We were sitting together at the bar."

"I thought... I felt." Bernadette frowned and put a hand to her forehead.

"You're going?" Rocky asked.

"I am," Jeremy said, glancing nervously over his shoulder. "It's too creepy here. I feel like something bad is going to happen. I'm getting out. Now." With that, he shook hands with them both and, picking up his duffle bag, crossed the lobby to the big glass door leading to the circular drive.

"There goes another loose end," Rocky said in frustration. "Just when I think we are getting somewhere with this case, it fizzles out."

Bernadette closed her eyes for a moment and shook her head, as if to clear it. "I thought something had happened to him." She turned to Rocky. "Now what? Feel like another drink?"

"Not really. I think I'd rather go back to our hotel. I have an early morning tomorrow at Passero's shop."

"Fine with me," Bernadette said. "I don't feel like sitting with Matty Dean again."

Rocky put a hand on the small of her back as they walked to the hotel entrance. Although he didn't think they were in any danger, he felt protective of her. He could see she was feeling a bit ...off.

The doorman held the heavy plate-glass door open for them, and they stepped outside. Jeremy was still there, scanning the cars parked on the edge of the circular drive, probably looking for a cab.

Then three things happened at once, although it felt like it was in slow motion as Rocky helplessly watched it unfold.

A cab pulled up on the far side of the wide, covered drive-through and Jeremy stepped off the curb onto the drive, raising a hand to hail it.

Just then a green station wagon shot out of the parking area, heading straight for him.

Before Rocky could react, Bernadette let out a low moan and slumped against his arm.

It was over in a moment. The thump, then the sound of the car speeding away, leaving Jeremy in a crumpled heap on the road.

Bernadette was out cold, and if Rocky hadn't already had his hand on her back, she would have fallen to the ground.

The doorman was running to Jeremy as Rocky sat Bernadette on the curb, glad to see she was coming around.

"You okay?" he asked, frowning at her intently.

She put a hand to her forehead. "Yes. What happened."

He glanced over to where the doorman was kneeling by the figure on the ground. "I think Jeremy is dead."

Chapter 40

M inutes later, lights flashing, siren wailing, a police vehicle pulled up to the curb between where Jeremy's body still lay on the drive, and where Rocky and Bernadette sat on the curb. The police turned off the siren, but the lights kept flashing, taking Rocky back to his time with the SFPD, a time he would rather forget.

The tinted window rolled down slowly and Niccolo's face appeared. He wasn't smiling. He was wearing what Rocky thought of as his Police Inspector's Face.

"What are you two doing here?"

Rocky gave a one shoulder shrug. His other arm was around Bernadette. She'd stopped shaking, but leaned against him, turning down offers by both the door attendant and the manager to come to a more comfortable seat in the lobby while they waited for the police to decide what would happen next.

Niccolo stepped out of the car. Seeing that the coroner was already inspecting the crime scene, he came over to Rocky and Bernadette and crouched down in front of them. "Is she okay."

"I'm okay," Bernadette said, straightening her shoulders and standing up. Niccolo stepped closer to prevent the hotel manager from overhearing their conversation.

"Is this connected with Hamish's death?" he asked quietly in English.

Rocky replied. "Seems to be,"

Niccolo's eyes narrowed. "I see, but I still need to know how you are connected - two murder scenes and you are at each one. Anyone else would say it was suspicious. Let me get witness statements and speak to the coroner, then we will talk."

The manager stepped forward and introduced himself to Niccolo, assuring him that he would do all he could to hurry the process along. Wanting, Rocky was sure, to get the body away from the hotel entrance as quickly as possible.

"I think I would like to go inside now, please," Bernadette said.

Probably a good idea. It was going to be a long night, and the temperature outside was dropping quickly.

"Certainly. You can use my office." The manager glanced back and forth between Niccolo and Rocky for their agreement. He was eager to help, perhaps sensing a more than professional relationship between the American witnesses and the Italian Ispettore.

Once Rocky and Bernadette were settled in his sumptuous office with coffee and cakes, he excused himself to go back to the crime scene.

As soon as the door closed, Bernadette asked, "What happened?"

Rocky squinted at her. "You don't remember?"

She shook her head. "Not really." Holding the cup with both hands, she brought it to her lips. Her eyes looked large over the rim.

"The car came right at him. Fast. Like it was waiting for him to come out. He didn't have a chance."

"Did you recognize it, the car?"

Rocky nodded slowly. "I think I've seen it before. At Fanucci's the night of the opening of Mondo Musica. It was the only other beat-up old car in the parking area. It's bigger than most of the cars in town, so it stands out. I think it's a Lada. A Russian station wagon."

"I haven't noticed many station wagons in town," Bernadette mused.

Rocky nodded. "It's not an Italian thing."

"So, Jeremy was right," Bernadette said slowly. "Someone *was* after him. Was it because he was going to accuse Fanucci of selling him a fake instrument? Is that worth killing for?"

"There could be more than one instrument involved. Fanucci's entire world – and he seems to have built a small empire here if his house is anything to go by – could come tumbling down around him. There could be any number of people working on this," Rocky said. "Like that Mafioso guy that's Fanucci's friend. Cassiglio. The guy Jeremy said sold him his violin. I don't think that's a coincidence."

"But would the Police Commissioner be friends with Fanucci if he's a crook?"

"Cremona is really just a small town. Loyalties can go way back."

"I guess the Commissioner might not know," Bernadette speculated.

But Rocky had his suspicions. During their Mexican debacle, he knew Bernadette thought he was overly distrustful of the police, so now he just said, "He might not know exactly what's going on, but corruption runs deep in Italy. The mafia has infiltrated most official offices and many officials are on their pay. The government is trying to dig out the corruption, but there is still a lot out there. Two years ago in Piacenza, just across the river, they uncovered a drug ring in an office of the Carabinieri, Italy's military police force. Seven officers were arrested for drug pushing and extortion. Grassi might well know what's going on in Cremona but not be in a position to stop it. Or might not want to stop it."

There was a knock on the door and Niccolo entered.

"That was quick," Rocky said.

Niccolo's look hardened. "The TPC showed up, again. They are taking *this* case away from our office, too. Yes, and before you ask, the deceased was carrying a violin, but we have no way of knowing if this event is connected to Hamish's murder."

"Is his violin all right?" Bernadette asked.

Niccolo shook his head. "Smashed beyond repair."

A look passed between Rocky and Bernadette. *Conveniently destroyed.*

Niccolo caught the look. His eyes narrowed even further. "What is it? What do you know?"

"We have reason to believe this *may* be connected to Hamish's death," Rocky said cautiously. He did not want to get his cousin in trouble by disclosing too much.

"What reason?" Niccolo asked sharply.

Rocky pulled the list of names out of his pocket and handed it to his cousin. "We found this in Hamish's room."

"How did you find it? We searched that room. TPC searched that room." His expression darkened even more. "And what exactly were you doing in his room?"

"We were following up on our own. Like you said," Rocky reminded him, ignoring the last question. Would he have shown Niccolo the list if his cousin were still on the case? He wasn't sure.

Niccolo studied the list, confusion replacing his anger. "Who are these people? And what do they have to do with any of it?"

"Jeremy Reynolds, the man who was just killed, is on that list," Bernadette said.

"Hmmph," Niccolo huffed, folded the list and tucked it in his shirt pocket. "I will keep this," he said officiously.

Rocky nodded. They didn't need the actual list. The names were firmly fixed in his mind and Bernadette had written all the information in her notebook.

"But what did Jeremy have to do with your friend Hamish?" Niccolo asked.

"We *think* Hamish was investigating violin forgeries."

"Fakes. That is possible. Was Jeremy Reynolds involved in this also?"

"We think so." Rocky trusted his cousin, but even if Niccolo was off the case, he didn't want to give their whole hand away and be tripping over cops every time they wanted to talk to a suspect.

Bernadette was watching the exchange carefully, but luckily she was following his lead and letting him handle it.

Niccolo regarded him with pinched lips for a moment, then blew out an exasperated breath. "Again, my hands are tied up. I can do nothing. But you two," he pointed first at Rocky then at Bernadette. "Be careful. These guys are not fooling around."

"Who are the police looking at?" Bernadette asked.

"There is a crime ring in Cremona. A branch of the Milan based 'ndrangheta mafia group know as the Valle clan."

Bernadette shook her head. "When I think of Milan I think of fashion, not mafia."

"These days it is both. In fact, it is the major center for drugs entering the country now, as well as many other related crimes. Milano, Brescia, and even Cremona. There have been many arrests in recent years, some involving government officials. Even within the *Guardia di Finanza*."

Rocky's brows rose. "The Financial Police?"

Niccolo nodded. "So, I repeat. Do not interfere. Keep your clean noses out of this. And now, the officer of the *Carabiniere* would like to speak with you."

Chapter 41

It was past two o'clock in the morning before Rocky and Bernadette got back to their hotel. Although she was exhausted, Bernadette was glad when Rocky invited her to his room for a nightcap. She was wired from the strong coffee they'd been drinking at the Continental, and they still hadn't had a chance to talk about Jeremy's murder.

She sank into one of the two chairs at the small desk, while Rocky went into the bathroom for fresh glasses and returned with a bottle of wine.

"Zio Ernesto's finest," he said, holding up the bottle for her inspection. It was dusty and missing a label, but when he poured it into the bathroom tumblers, it was the color of rubies.

The taste did not disappoint either. Bernadette rolled the first sip around in her mouth for a moment, to fully appreciate the flavor, then she swallowed. As the warmth spread through her body, her shoulders finally relaxed.

She gave a little shudder and sat back in her chair. "So the TPC – who are they again?"

"The Art Police. An arm of the *Carabinieri*."

She shook her head. "You weren't kidding when you said the police system here is complicated. And they can just move in and take over the case?"

Rocky shrugged. "They are the Military Police. Nicco's office is just local."

Bernadette sighed. "*So* complicated. Financial police, art police, military police. What could they be looking for?"

"Well, the financial police might be looking for smuggling, or money laundering. The art police would be looking for art theft, or in this case, theft of a violin."

"Or a violin forgery?"

"Possibly. But it sounds like we know as much as they do at this point."

"That *Carabinieri* officer was intense." She glanced at Rocky's face but couldn't read his expression. His gaze was fixed on the glass on the table, so she continued. "Maybe Nicco is right. Maybe we should let the police handle it."

Rocky took a minute to answer, as if he was making up his mind about something, then he looked her in the eye and said, "He was more than my friend. I owed him my life."

Finally, the story! Bernadette sat quietly, hardly breathing.

Rocky seemed to withdraw, go somewhere deep inside, the fingers of one hand turning his glass on the table.

"I met Hamish in Aleppo, Syria," he said in a low voice. "He was a reporter and I was a photographer for the foreign press. It was a dangerous time. The city was a war zone. That's why we were there, recording the horrors of war for papers and magazines back home.

"Smoke drifted through the streets, mixed with the dust of crumbling buildings. Sometimes you had to walk around bodies sprawled across the sidewalk, waiting for the family to find them and carry them away. One bombing at a market was even worse. All that was left there were body parts." He shook his head. "But the grizzlier the better, as far as the papers were concerned."

His eyes looked glazed, and Bernadette sensed he was seeing it all again. "It was hell. The streets were always deserted. We crept along, as close to the buildings as possible, trying to stay out of the sightlines of snipers who you couldn't see from the street, but who were waiting in the bombed-out buildings for an unsuspecting target."

Rocky stared into his glass. "I was drinking too much. Every evening I went to this local bar around the corner from my hotel. A small hole-in-the-wall – with literal holes in the walls from a mortar attack. That's where I met Jasmine. She was a reporter whose home was Aleppo, and who was passionate about the struggle. She had been married, but her husband had joined the rag-tag militia. Differences in their ideals had driven them apart.

"The second night, she took me up to her room, a single room on the third floor above the bar. The bathroom, such as it was, was down the hall. I spent a few nights there, listening to her quiet stories while we lay together on a bare mattress on the floor."

Bernadette could see it, smell it, vividly.

"It helped, spending time with her. I was struggling, but she made me feel that maybe I could do the job. Maybe it was worth doing. The fourth night, we heard someone run up the stairs and then pound on the door. Jasmine's eyes went wide with fear. 'Amir,' she whispered. Her husband.

"But then I heard Hamish's voice through the door. 'Rocky. You've got to get out of here. Her husband's coming.'

"I jumped up, pulled on my pants, and opened the door. Hamish was standing in the dark hallway, alone. He looked worried, kept looking over his shoulder as if he expected someone to be right on his heals. I looked back at Jasmine, and I remember she was sitting up, pulling a tee shirt over her head. Then, she ruffled her hair." Rocky closed his eyes and Bernadette could see he was there, remembering the time, the place, the woman.

He sighed deeply, then looked at her and smiled sadly. "She had such beautiful black hair." A frown creased his forehead as he searched for the thread of the story. Finally, he continued. "Then she shrugged and said, 'You go. I can handle Amir.'

"Standing in the hall, we heard noise on the street – unusual with the strict evening curfew – so I grabbed my jacket and shoes, gave her one last kiss, and ran out the door.

"She called after us, 'Take the fire escape. At the back.' Then Hamish shut the door and as we raced down the hall, I heard Jasmine turn the lock behind us.

"A window at the far end of the hall opened onto a fire escape. We climbed out and crept as silently as possible down the creaky old iron staircase. Men's voices echoed out the open window from the hallway above. It sounded like they went the other way, towards Jasmine's room." He shook his head. "I prayed she'd be all right.

"We jumped the last eight feet to the stony alleyway, God that hurt, but then I glanced up and saw a face peer out the window. The man yelled something to the others and before we could move, a bullet hit the wall beside my head, sending stone fragments flying." He unconsciously touched a small scar on his temple. "We raced down the alleyway dodging the round of automatic machine gun fire that *pinged* off the iron staircase on the next building, over our heads.

"I don't know how we made it to the end of that alley, but when we turned the corner, the street was dark and quiet. We ran to my hotel, half a block away.

"In my room, we collapsed and caught our breath. I grabbed two warm beers out of the mini-fridge – it never did work – and we toasted our narrow escape. I thanked Hamish for finding me – he didn't have to – and I told him I was done. Done with the job and done with the life.

"'I'm getting too old for this,' I said, and Hamish said he was, too. 'Let's call it quits,' he said. 'We can get out of here tomorrow.' We clinked our beer bottles to seal the pact.

"We lined up tickets for the next morning and barely made it to the airport in time for our flight, and then only by paying the cab driver a hostage ransom."

He stopped for a minute and stared at the table. Bernadette could see that the next part was hard for him to say. She cringed in preparation.

"Minutes before we boarded the plane, I saw the headline in the morning paper. *JOURNALIST FOUND MURDERED IN HER BED.*"

Bernadette closed her eyes. "Oh, Rocky."

He shook his head, landing hard in the present, his eyes, dark wounds. She couldn't bear to see him looking this vulnerable.

After a minute, she blew out a ragged sigh, raised her head and threw back her shoulders. "I guess we'd better figure out who killed Hamish."

Rocky sagged in his chair. Whether from relief at getting the story out or that she agreed to continue, she didn't know. But it didn't matter.

Now, they had work to do.

She opened her notebook and ran her finger down Hamish's list of names. "Gustaf is the only one we know of who's here." She closed her book with a snap. "Tomorrow we'll find him and see what he knows about Gretta Webber. The other name on the list."

Saturday, Day Five

Chapter 42

The following morning Rocky arose before dawn. He and Bernadette had agreed to work on their own and meet at the hotel at ten o'clock. He grabbed a quick coffee at the hotel restaurant as it opened its doors.

"*Mi dispiace*," the young server apologised that the pastries were yet to be laid out. But the espresso machine was steaming and Rocky assured her that all he needed was a quick, extra strong double espresso, which she was happy to make.

When he was on a job, Rocky always got up early to take photos, in this case of the angled sun glinting off dew-soaked metal railings and shop windows. To record piazzas and narrow lanes before the crowds arrived, the low light highlighting the texture of the cobblestone streets and ancient walls. He liked nothing better than to catch a lone cyclist, or a cat silhouetted against a crumbling wall in the warm morning light.

Two hours later, when the morning rush invaded the streets, he grabbed another coffee and a pastry in a small *cafeteria* across from Piazza Roma, and at nine o'clock met Mia at Passero's shop.

She waved him in from her perch up on a low cabinet where she was unscrewing a light fixture from the wall. "*Il maestro* says the booth is too dark," she said, placing the fixture in a box and climbing down. "I asked him, though, and he said you could stay here alone and take pictures. Are you coming to the *Fiera* later?"

"Yes, I am. When I'm finished here I'll swing by the hotel and get Bernadette and we'll come to the show. How do I lock up?"

Mia pulled a ring of keys out of her pocket, peeled one off, and handed it to Rocky. "You can borrow my key. Signore Passero would like to speak with you, but this is the craziest weekend of the year. Are you staying next week?"

"For a few days. It's Bernadette who will interview him, though."

Mia grinned. "That's good. He likes the ladies. I'd better go or I will be late. He will want me to get these lights up before the fair opens at ten."

She grabbed her coat and hurried out the door, arms laden with the box of lights. Rocky closed the door and locked up after her. A small group of people had stopped in front of the shop and were peering hopefully through the window. He pointed to the closed sign hanging on the door and turned back into the shop.

He stood for a moment, taking in the silence. He could imagine the shop on a normal workday; musicians and teachers coming and going for strings and rosin, music soaring to the high ceiling as they tried violins, occasionally buying. But the street level store was virtually empty, all of the instruments on display at the trade show.

He climbed the open staircase that hugged the brick wall and stepped into the cavernous workshop at the top of the stairs. He stood quietly, assessing the space, absorbing the atmosphere, and breathing in the earthy aroma of freshly planed wood and the intoxicating tang of linseed oil and varnish.

On a normal workday, apprentices would be busy at the benches where instruments now lay abandoned in various stages of completion, casting interesting shadows in the low morning light that streamed in through the window over Passero's bench. Rocky set up his tripod and affixed his camera on top, focussing on a row of handmade knives and chisels hanging above one of the old, gnarled benches. Planes of all sizes lined the back of the bench, some so small they would fit in the palm of one hand. One still sat on the bench, a curled ribbon of shaved wood by its side. He zoomed in for a closeup. Perfect.

He moved his tripod to Passero's bench, his footsteps raising a fine haze of sawdust that spangled the air in a shaft of sunlight pouring in through the big, semi-circular window. He stood, as the master would, looking down on the street, now a sea of bicycles and people on foot who at this time on a Saturday morning were probably heading to work in the shops or to the market or the park. This vantage point was perfect for keeping an eye on the comings and going of the town, as well as who was visiting Fanucci's shop next door.

Rocky's mind wandered back to last night, when they'd been standing in front of Passero's shop waiting for Mia to lock up. Fanucci had obviously been open for business because despite the hour, people had been coming and going. That was probably a dealer's life. Especially during Mondo Musica. They would have to be ready anytime anyone wanted to do business. The bigger question was, had Jay been buying or selling? Or both? Trading up? He'd openly stated he hoped to acquire a Certificate of Authenticity for his violin on this trip. And a better violin.

A flaming pink coat caught his eye amongst the people walking through the park, reminding him that Mirela, too, had been in the vicinity the night before. Now she emerged from the tree cover and crossed the street, heading directly toward him. He peered down but couldn't tell which door she disappeared into. Passero's shop was closed, he'd locked the door behind Mia himself, so it had to either be the door to the stairs to Passero's private apartment above or the door to Fanucci's shop next door.

Rocky stopped and listened, and a moment later heard footsteps in the flat above. He looked at the rough wooden ceiling boards overhead. What was she doing here again? But the fact that Mirela was up there probably meant Passero was, too.

Rocky suddenly felt uncomfortable and wondered if Passero could hear him, as well. Not the time to do any more exploring. He'd have to find another time. It was hard to come up with a clear motive for Passero to murder Hamish, but he was one of the last people to see him alive and was definitely involved somehow. If he could only get into Passero's private quarters, he might find some answers.

He was finished taking photographs for now and as silently as possible, let himself out of the store. Then he walked back to the hotel to meet Bernadette.

Chapter 43

"I was hoping we could meet Gustaf at the farm this morning," Bernadette said, sadly eyeing yet another dry breakfast pastry.

"You'll have to wait," Rocky said with a grin. "We'll be going to the farm for dinner tonight. In the meantime, we have a lot to do. We are falling behind on our work for the magazine. We still have to interview Tatiana; there's the final concert coming up–"

"–and I still have to meet Giovanni at the Archaeology Museum." Bernadette felt her cheeks flush foolishly at the thought.

"Right. That should be fun."

"Oh, come on, Rocky. I'm going to try to get another piece on the Tacitus dig in *Archaeology* magazine." She raised her eyebrows. "I hope you got some good pictures to go with it."

"Of course," he said indignantly.

She hid a smile. He was always grumpy when the tables were turned and *she* questioned if *he* was prepared. That was usually his trick.

"I'll come, but I might not stay for the whole tour of the museum."

"That's okay. I wouldn't want to bore you. I'd like to go into the cathedral, too. The *Duomo*," she amended. "And up the tower. The view must be incredible."

Rocky downed his cappuccino. "First let's go to Mondo Musica and hunt down Gustaf."

When they got to the arena, the doors had just opened and few visitors roamed the aisles. Makers and dealers stood at the corners of their booths, chatting to their neighbors. Apprentices were dusting and polishing the instruments.

They found Gustaf sitting in his booth, reading over some papers. When they approached, he motioned for them to take the two chairs on the other side of his desk.

"Hello my friends. Are you enjoying the festival?"

Bernadette smiled at his enthusiasm. "Very entertaining," she agreed, then sobered. "But have you heard? There has been another murder."

Gustaf's smile fell into a concerned frown. "Yes. I heard on the Twitter."

Bernadette winced. She hated the way a crime became viral, with anyone and everyone having a comment to make.

"And it was Jeremy!" Gustaf exclaimed. His bushy eyebrows pulled together in a frown. "Did you talk to him? It wasn't connected to Amos's death, was it?"

"I'm afraid it might have been," Rocky said. "We spoke to Jeremy yesterday afternoon and he said he knew Amos. Together they had planned to approach someone about a violin Jeremy bought here in Cremona a few years ago which he had since been told was a forgery. But when Amos was murdered, Jeremy got spooked. He decided to call the whole thing off and was on his way out of town last night when he was hit by a car. The police are calling it suspicious."

Gustaf nodded thoughtfully. "I will take your warning to be careful more seriously now. Who would have thought...here...?"

"What can you tell us about Gretta Webber?" Bernadette asked impatiently.

"Ah," Gustaf leaned back in his chair, hands linked on his ample belly. "Interestingly, Gretta had that exact same problem – she bought a violin here and later I had to tell her it was not what she thought. Not a Tommaso Balestrieri, but a lesser-known maker of that same period whose work had been modified to resemble one."

"Modified? How?" Rocky asked.

"Passing one instrument off as another is much easier when the violin is of the same era. Gretta's was nicely aged of course, an expert job, made of old wood, although not as good quality as the maple and spruce Balestrieri would have used. Her violin was newer by fifty or even one-hundred years, and possibly had been made as a Balestrieri copy to begin with. It may already have had an old, forged label in it. But any unscrupulous maker or dealer, someone with a sharp eye and out to make some money, would have seen it for what it was, a fake. They could have bought it, turned around and sold it to an unsuspecting young buyer like Gretta for more than it was worth."

"How much more?" Bernadette asked.

"In this case, possibly two hundred thousand Euros more."

Bernadette gasped.

He sighed. "But by then, it is too late. The deal is done. A good copy and, who knows?" He shrugged. "Maybe the dealer did not know. You can understand how upset Gretta was when I told her. But at least the violin came with papers of authenticity that most people would accept."

"But not you," Rocky said.

"No, not me. And I felt it was my duty to tell her what I thought. Anything else would have been unethical."

"Who did she buy the violin from?" Bernadette asked.

Gustaf's expression tightened. "I would rather not say."

Bernadette could understand his reticence. With two murders this week already, he had good reason to be cautious.

But Rocky didn't let it go. "Let me ask you this. Did she buy it here from Fanucci?"

Gustaf glanced past them into the crowd that was beginning to form in his booth, then back at Rocky. "I cannot say."

But Gustaf's reticence to clear Fanucci's name spoke volumes, and Bernadette felt sure Gretta had bought the violin from him. "When was this?" she asked.

"Two years ago," Gustaf replied. "The last time she was here."

"Is she here this year?" Bernadette asked.

"I think not," Gustaf said. Then he muttered under his breath, "I hope not."

"Thank you, sir," Rocky said, standing to leave and holding out his hand to shake. "I think we've got what we need."

It was Saturday morning and the arena was already packed. For a reason unknown to Bernadette, Rocky led them the long way around to the exit, past Passero's booth where both Mia and Passero were busy with customers. Bernadette shot Rocky a slant-eyed look, that he ignored. What was he up to now?

Chapter 44

As they exited the Fiera, Bernadette looked back over her shoulder. "Even though our names aren't on Hamish's list, I have a creepy feeling we are being watched."

Rocky glanced at her, trying to gage her expression and saw she was serious and slightly pale. Always a bad sign with Bernadette.

"That's enough detecting," he said, hoping a change of subject would ease her mind. "Time to get back to the work we are here for."

"Right," she said, her tone immediately lighter. "I have that meeting with Giovanni at noon. I said we would meet him at the entrance to the Archaeological Museum."

"Where is that?" Rocky asked.

"It's in a decommissioned church, *Chiesa San Lorenzo*, quite close to the hotel."

They parked the Cinquecento at the hotel and Rocky said, "You go ahead to the museum. I'll meet you there later. And remember, we are expected at the farm for dinner tonight."

"What are you going to do in the meantime?"

"I'm going to track down who sent the broken violin to Tatiana."

Remembering what the desk clerk had told him, it didn't take long for Rocky to find the hole-in-the-wall courier service who had delivered the box to the hotel. And it didn't take too many Euros to find out who had sent it – Gloria, Jay's handler, interesting information Rocky tucked away before heading to Passero's shop.

Since he'd seen Passero less than an hour before at the Fiera, he felt fairly confident that both the shop and the apartment above would be empty. He still had Mia's key, so he let himself in and headed up the stairs.

On the workshop floor, he paused and listened for sounds of footsteps overhead. On his previous visits, it had been obvious from the creaking floorboards overhead that someone was up there. Now the building was silent. The only sound was muffled traffic noise from the street below.

Even so, Rocky walked softly up the second flight of stairs. They were anchored to the brick wall and open to the lofty workshop below, but considerably narrower than the first flight. There was a landing at the top, outside the door to Passero's inner sanctum. He put his ear to the door and listened, but heard nothing within. To be sure, he knocked boldly on the scarred wooden door. Again, nothing.

He tried Mia's key in the door but as he suspected, it didn't fit. In the dim light he could see that this was a much older lock in a much older, wooden door. He pulled the pick set out of his pocket and got to work.

The lock was at least fifty years old. It took less than a minute before the door swung open. Rocky glanced over his shoulder at the empty workshops below, then stepped inside.

This floor was the attic, with high sloped ceilings inset with dusty dormer windows. The whole place was covered in a thin layer of sawdust, generated at Passero's workbench, which was situated, like in the workshop below, in front of a window overlooking the street. A sink stood in the front corner and, from the look of the dishes and varnish brushes soaking there, doubled as both a workshop and kitchen sink. A dark area at the rear of the large room was set up as sleeping quarters with a bed, dresser, and an old recliner. A bachelor pad. Kind of sad, Rocky thought. A far, *far,* cry from Fanucci's villa. If anyone was making money on this scheme – the forgery ring that was beginning to take shape in Rocky's head – it certainly wasn't the Maestro.

He studied the workshop area looking for clues as to Passero's part in it all. Anything he might have used to age violins. But with his limited knowledge of the trade, Rocky wasn't sure what he was looking for. He was afraid he'd have to ask Mia for help, but she seemed devoted to Passero and would probably balk at breaking into his private workshop.

Rocky snapped a few shots of the workbench area and felt surprisingly uncomfortable doing so. Then, with one final glance around, let himself out.

Time to meet Bernadette at the museum.

Rocky was disconcerted to find Bernadette head-to-head with the archeologist, Giovanni Presutti, deep in conversation over a display of pre-Roman pot sherds. But her guileless smile of greeting reassured him he wasn't intruding, that there was nothing going on between them.

Of course not. The man was old enough to be her father!

Giovanni greeted Rocky graciously, then said it was time he got back to work, giving Bernadette the customary double cheek kiss and shaking Rocky's hand as he left.

As usual, Bernadette was excited by the scraps of broken pottery in the glass case and happy to explain their significance to Rocky. Although it was a subject that usually didn't hold his interest, he was surprised how content he was to listen to Bernadette and how ready he was to give her all the time she needed. As she spoke, he took shots of the broken pieces of pottery and of the interior of the museum in case she did come up with another archaeological article once they got home.

The ancient, thirteenth century church was really quite beautiful. Although it had been retrofitted to house museum displays of Roman and medieval artifacts, the designer had managed to make the original Romanesque features of the church look modern and minimalist, while maintaining the mysterious atmosphere of the Middle Ages.

When Bernadette was finally finished scribbling notes in her omnipresent notebook, she turned to Rocky with a grin. "Done."

"Great," he said and, taking her hand, they headed for the door. "Time to go to the farm."

Chapter 45

Rocky's shoulders relaxed as the Cinquecento bounced through the pastoral Lombardi country-side heading to the family farm. The last few days had been rough. He needed this break. With the late afternoon sun shining through the open hatch in the roof and Bernadette by his side, this was exactly the scenario he'd hoped he could arrange, a chance to show Bernadette more of family life at Castello Maria. Tonight some of his cousins would be there, including Nicco and Mia. Hopefully, they could find a quiet moment to update each other on the case.

He turned in through the off-kilter iron gate at the farm, making a lap around the courtyard and parking in front of the main house. Once out of the car though, as promised, he steered Bernadette toward the modern barn to meet 'the girls,' the gentle, doe-eyed Brune, the Italian brown cows that were waiting patiently in their stalls. Zio Ernesto waved from the back of the barn, and Rocky could see the evening milking was about to begin. So after giving the girls pats on their soft noses, he led Bernadette outside and into the small family cheese shop next door.

The cheese shop was all business. A spotless stainless-steel worktable ran along the back wall and a glass fronted cooler held tubs of pure white mozzarella floating in brine and deliciously mouldy rounds of hard cheese that Rocky told Bernadette had aged in the castello cellar. When he'd lived at the farm, he often spent afternoons working in the store and had enjoyed meeting neighbors who stopped in on their way home from work to buy cheese and sausage for the next day's lunch. He felt a strangely elemental satisfaction from cutting into the big, firm rounds of cheese with the cleavers Ernesto kept razor sharp. It made him feel he was an important part of the family.

Now, Zia Sophia stood behind the glass case, greeting him and Bernadette with, "ciao's," and offering slices from one of the soft, creamy, raw milk cheeses Castello Maria specialized in. Bernadette moaned her appreciation, making both him and Sophia smile. His aunt must have been waiting for their arrival, because after a few short minutes of rapid-fire questions in Italian – she'd heard through the family grapevine about his connection to "the murdered stranger" – Sophia removed her apron, hung it on a hook behind the counter and ushered them out the door.

"We should write a piece about this place," Bernadette said excitedly as they made their way to the smaller courtyard and the family entrance of the castello.

"We could," he agreed. "You find us the job and I'll supply the background info."

Sophia disappeared into the house ahead of them, but as they hung up their jackets in the foyer, they were assailed by a complex, mouth-watering aroma so thick Rocky could almost taste it. Tomato, strong cheese and, hovering beneath it all, garlic and onion.

Sophia was stirring a large pot on the stove when they entered the kitchen and she started to speak before they got through the door. She spoke little or no English and Bernadette knew virtually no Italian, although she had managed a nice formal greeting that Rocky could see pleased his aunt. Somehow, though, the two women seemed to understand each other in what had always seemed to him to be a psychic way that women have with each other. Bernadette asked simple one-word questions about every dish, and Sophia was pleased to explain, even putting her to work assembling an antipasto platter from the salami, cheese and marinated vegetables that were already sitting out on the island.

His aunt put Rocky to work as well, setting the long harvest table in the breakfast room and lighting candles to supplement the rudimentary electrical lights. Then, as his cousins began to arrive, he played host, fixing Paola a Negroni cocktail made of Campari, sweet Vermouth and gin, and an Aperol spritz for Valentina. Then Bernadette came into the dining hall bearing the groaning antipasto platter. Rocky helped her set it on the table, stealing a thin slice of soppressata salami for his trouble.

"You remember Valentina from the breakfast," he said, coaching Bernadette, who seemed slightly overwhelmed by the warm double-cheek kiss his cousin gave her. Then he poured her a glass of Prosecco before both she and Valentina disappeared back into the kitchen.

When Charlie and Leonardo and their wives and children arrived, the noise level doubled and the party began.

Replete from the meal of creamy risotto and ossobuco, Bernadette sat back, enjoying the slightly protective curve of Rocky's arm across the back of her chair, a shield in this large, boisterous crowd of Falconis. The younger people, like Nicco and Valentina, spoke English well, but the older generation was not as bilingual. Rocky often dipped in close to translate something that was being said, and her insides warmed at the feel of his breath in her ear.

Stracciatella gelato that Ernesto had made from cream from the creamery followed the meal, accompanied by Amaretti cookies and a small glass of Limoncello, provided by Leonardo and his wife.

Bernadette could feel a flush on her cheeks from the wine and warmth of the room. She turned to Rocky, smiled and said, "I don't know why you ever left. The food is amazing, and the people are so friendly."

"I didn't want to work on the farm," he said. "The wide world was calling." A soft smile lifted one corner of his mouth. "But you're right, it is pretty special."

Bernadette was enjoying this easy-going side of her partner that had surfaced on this Italian trip whenever his family was involved. But then she felt him stiffen beside her as Niccolo caught his eye from down the table. His cousin walked out the glass doors at the end of the dining hall and, moments later, Rocky gave Bernadette's hand a squeeze and followed with Bernadette close behind.

Outside, the cool breeze felt good on Bernadette's over-heated cheeks. The air smelled like rain was coming as they settled on the steps to the old servants' quarters.

"Is there any news about Jeremy's murder?" Rocky asked.

Nicco gave him a side glance as he lit a cigarette. "I have heard that the violin was not what the label said it was."

"I thought you were off the case," Rocky said.

Nicco shrugged one shoulder. "The TPC have taken over offices in our building. The walls are thin."

Bernadette mulled over the information about the violin. "How can they tell it was a fake? Wasn't it destroyed in the accident?"

"Yes, it is in pieces, but an expert can tell."

"Did they ask Fanucci?" Rocky asked.

"Ah, no." Niccolo glanced over his shoulder, then back to them. "No, we brought in an outside expert. This week in Cremona they are everywhere. Like fleas on the back of the dog."

Bernadette wondered if they had consulted Gustaf Braun.

"And this expert decided it was a fake," Rocky clarified.

"*Sì.*"

Rocky thought back to his last meeting with Gustaf and wondered who, other than Fanucci, would have papers good enough that Gustaf would hesitate to confront them.

"Why, besides the suspiciously coincidental timing, do you think Jeremy's murder was connected to Hamish's?" Niccolo asked.

Rocky looked at Bernadette, who looked back, wide eyed. He knew what she was thinking because he was wondering the same thing. Was it time to tell Niccolo everything? No, not quite. Not until they had proof.

"I don't know, *cugino*," Rocky said. "When I do you'll be the first to know."

Niccolo stubbed out his cigarette. "I hope so." He slapped Rocky on the shoulder and stood up. "In the meantime, be careful."

Meeting over.

Fat drops of rain splatted the cobbles at their feet as they headed indoors to say their goodbyes.

Chapter 46

A few minutes later, Rocky and Bernadette raced across the courtyard and scrambled into the Fiat. The rain was coming down hard now, heavy drops pelting their faces.

Once inside the car, Rocky wiped his wet cheeks with the sleeve of his jacket, then reached above their heads to close the hatch which had been stuck half-open since they'd borrowed the car. It hadn't mattered. He'd appreciated the ventilation, but now the rain was getting in. It was stuck, so he tugged it open and yanked it back, but no luck. In fact, he thought he'd lost a few inches in the process.

"Sorry. I think that's as good as it's going to get. I'll drive fast."

He took off out of the courtyard, the wind driving raindrops in through the hatch, quickly soaking their heads and shoulders. The creaky wipers fought to keep up with the deluge. Clouds covered the moon making visibility near zero. Leaning close to the windscreen, trying to see the dark road in the weak beam of the headlights, Rocky made a right turn onto another narrow, unmarked road.

"Are you sure you know where you're going?" Bernadette asked, clutching the handle on the dash.

"I could drive this road blindfolded."

"You might as well be."

Out the window, hulking shapes of dark buildings crowded the road as they passed through the village near the farm. Three streetlights illuminated the three blocks of town, then they were thrown back into the darkness.

A bar of light lit Rocky's eyes. He glanced in the rear-view mirror and muttered, "Turn down your high beams, buddy."

The car behind them pulled closer, right on their tail. Blinded by the light, he couldn't tell much about it, except that the car was big, much bigger than ninety per cent of the cars he'd seen since he'd been in Cremona. Far bigger than the Fiat.

"Do they want to pass?" Bernadette asked.

"I've pulled over as far as I can. On this straight stretch, they can pass if they want to."

It was hard enough to see the road in these conditions even without being blinded from behind. He glanced in the rear-view mirror again. "Asshole."

The headlights grew even brighter as the car approached, then suddenly dimmed.

Slam! The Fiat lurched ahead. Bernadette's head snapped back.

"What the hell!" They'd been rammed from behind!

Rocky gripped the wheel, both arms straight, trying to keep the car on the road. Beside him, Bernadette thrust her hands out to brace herself on the metal dashboard.

He shifted into high gear and hit the gas. The Cinque-cento hesitated for a moment as if pulling together its reserves, then surged ahead. Although he was sure their pursuers could catch their little Fiat, the other car dropped back, staying ten feet behind, stalking them.

"Brace yourself!" Rocky ordered, then yanked the steering wheel to the left. Bernadette was thrown against his shoulder as the car made a sharp turn onto a dirt road. Glancing in the mirror, he saw the other car's lights disappear. They'd missed the turn.

Rocky roared down the dark road, taking advantage of the moment's reprieve to gain a few hundred feet before he saw the lights make the corner behind them and resume the chase.

The other car gained on them quickly and out of the corner of his eye he saw Bernadette brace herself on the dashboard in preparation for another hit.

The sedan raced up and rammed them again. With the Fiat motor in the rear, he was surprised the little Cinque-cento kept on going. But it did.

Their pursuers must have been surprised too because they fell back again.

"We can't take many more hits like that."

"Who is it?" Bernadette asked in a surprisingly steady voice.

"I'm fairly sure it's the station wagon I've seen around town. It's always on the heels of trouble."

Rocky figured he might have one advantage. He knew exactly where they were, and what was coming. From the fact that their pursuers missed that last turn, he had to assume they didn't.

"Open the hatch right up," he yelled.

"Why?"

"Just do it."

Bernadette reached above their heads with both hands and pushed back the flap. Luckily, it moved because, just then, their lights caught the gleam of water ahead.

Their speed carried them ten feet into the Po. Icy water flooded in through the rusted floorboards and swirled around their feet. Then the engine died.

"Can you swim?" he asked.

"Varsity," she answered, unbuckling her seatbelt.

Their pursuers stopped with the sedan's front wheels in the water, bright headlights illuminating inside the Fiat.

The little car sank deeper, the current nudging them downstream. Dark water quickly circled their waists. Rocky's breath hitched as the frigid water hit his chest.

"I know this place," he said. "It's all low bank downstream but the brush is thick."

The freezing water felt like an iron band around his neck. "Don't fight the current. Edge your way to the shore."

He grabbed her hand and squeezed, trying to send her encouragement in the few seconds they had left. Hoping she didn't pick up on the desperation he felt.

The water rushed in, quickly filling the interior of the car. He managed one more deep breath before it swirled over his head. He felt a bounce, the car rocked for a moment, then settled on the bottom.

The river was a dark icy force that like the cold hands of death, held him pinned in his seat. Pulling together all his inner strength, he reached up and felt the ceiling. The hatch was clear.

Beside him he sensed Bernadette rise and slip through the flap. The current was strong, but she might make it. If she didn't panic.

As her feet slipped through, he followed her up, his feet pushing off first the seat, then the roof of the car. Seconds later he bobbed to the surface. He gulped air letting the force of the water carry him downstream. His stomach felt like a concrete block, threatening to pull him under again.

Behind him, the lights of the sedan shot out over the water. The men were out of the car. He could hear them shouting to each other, but he couldn't make out what they said. Then they disappeared as the current pulled him around a bend

All he could think of was finding Bernadette. He couldn't see her in that inky, water world. But he had to find her. He had to try.

Waves washed over his head and he swallowed a mouthful of the murky river. Choking and coughing, he took another deep breath and prepared to dive. But then he heard her voice over the rush of the water. "Rocky."

His muscles relaxed, and it was suddenly much easier to breath. His head swivelled in the direction of her voice. His eyes had adjusted to the darkness enough to make out her silhouette against the slight silvery sheen of the water. She bobbed along with the current not five feet away, between him and the black shoreline. He inched over to her and together they silently made their way toward safety.

Fifty feet downstream, they neared the shore, grabbing low branches to stop from being swept further down river. In another few weeks, the winter rains would start in earnest and the Po would surge with the influx of water from the mountains. Even now, the current was swift and the water icy.

They fought their way through the scrubby brush partially submerged at the already high waterline. Bernadette lost her footing and went under, but Rocky grabbed her hand, held her back against the current until she could stand again. She grabbed a young sapling submerged in the rising water, and they stumbled to shore.

The underbrush was thick. They would never make it out to the road but, for the moment, they were safe.

Bernadette sank to the ground. "Who are they?"

"Sh-h-h," Rocky said, waiting until he heard the car doors slam in the distance and the motor start and pull away before he answered.

"You know that green station wagon we've been seeing? I think it was them."

"But who are they?"

"I don't know."

Bernadette mulled this over in silence. The moon slipped out from behind the clouds and he could see her, sitting a few feet away, shivering on the muddy ground.

He pulled his phone out of the inner pocket of his jacket. At least he hadn't lost it in the water.

"That won't work," she said through chattering teeth.

He turned it on and was relieved to hear a signal.

"Seriously? Who are you, James Bond?"

Rocky chuckled. She was okay. Even when wet, cold, and half drowned, he could count on Bernadette for a snarky response.

He wiped the dripping phone against his wet jacket, then called Paola. He waited while it rang. "Isn't yours waterproof?"

Bernadette just shook her head.

Finally, his cousin answered. "*Pronto.*"

"Paola. I need you to pick us up. With the boat. We're on the river."

He gave her directions, ended the call, then moved over to sit beside Bernadette. She was shivering violently so he put his arm around her.

"Share the warmth," he said, and pulled her close. Then all they could do was wait.

Chapter 47

Fifteen minutes later, the dark hulking shape of a boat chugged into view, cruising slowly on the deceptively silky water, panning a light into the thick brush that lined the shore. Rocky put a hand on Bernadette's arm to still her. Then he heard Paola's voice call, "Rocky?"

He jumped to his feet, pulling Bernadette up with him. Sprinting the fifteen feet to the waterline, he splashed in up to his knees, waving his arms.

Paola saw him. Fighting the current that threatened to spin the boat around, she nosed the bow into the brush ten feet away. Niccolo leaned over the gunwale, grabbing a partially submerged sapling to hold them in place.

Rocky and Bernadette scrambled over the bristly shrubs and logs floating in the shallows to reach the boat, then Paola shone the torch to the bow and Niccolo held out a strong hand to haul Bernadette up over the side. Paola draped a woollen blanket over Bernadette's shoulders as Rocky clambered into the boat and, seconds later, they were roaring full tilt back in the direction from which the boat had come. Back to Castello Maria.

The rain had stopped by the time they pulled up to the dock, and the moon broke through the clouds. Zio Ernesto was waiting, arms crossed on his chest, and Bernadette's jaw dropped as she realized in horror that they had drowned Ernesto's car in the Po.

But he knelt and caught the rope Nicco threw to him, securing the boat to iron rings on the dock. Then, without a word, he helped Bernadette and Rocky out of the boat. The old farm truck was waiting on the dirt road at the end of the pier. Rocky and Bernadette sat in the cab with Ernesto, and Niccolo and Paola climbed into the bed of the truck. In silence, they rode to the farm.

When they staggered into the castello kitchen, dripping a trail of river water along the brick floor, Zia Sophia broke the silence with a barrage of questions. Bernadette didn't know what she was saying, but allowed the motherly woman to lead her to a nearby bedroom where a warm change of clothes was laid out on the bed. Sophia turned on a steaming shower in the adjoining bathroom and indicated Bernadette should wash off the river muck and put on the clean clothes.

After the most appreciated shower of her life, Bernadette finally stopped shivering. She pulled on the wool sweater and too-long pants – so much too long that she knew they must belong to Paola. Then she looked in the mirror. Her hair hung wet around her face, but not wanting to overdo her welcome by rummaging around in the bathroom for a hairdryer and comb, she decided this would have to do.

When she emerged she found Rocky, washed and dressed, deep in conversation with Niccolo, describing the details of the drive from the farm to their final destination in the river. Then they all lapsed into thoughtful silence.

Finally, Zio Ernesto spoke up. "I courted your aunt in that car."

Rocky closed his eyes and shook his head. "*Mi dispiace, Tio.* I'm sorry. I didn't know…"

Ernesto waved away his apology. "Not your fault. Maybe we can pull it out in the spring."

They drank hot espresso liberally laced with grappa, a drink Sophia called *caffe cornetto* that Bernadette had heard of but had never thought she'd try. Now, though, it hit the spot. The extra piece of *Torta du Amaretti* didn't hurt either.

Mia arrived while they were eating, having worked the evening shift at Mondo Musica.

She flopped in a chair at the table, picked up a piece of cake with her fingers and wolfed it down, waving off Sophia's offer of a plate of dinner's leftovers. "*No, grazie.* I ate. Sort of." She took another piece of cake, then turned to Rocky. "The Maestro asked for you to go by and see him."

"Passero?" Rocky asked.

She nodded, her mouth full of cake.

"What about?"

"I don't know," she said. "He seemed sort of… agitated."

Bernadette sighed when she saw Rocky was wearing his stone-faced cop look, but she knew enough to wait until they were alone to find out what he thought Passero wanted to say.

When Niccolo ushered them out the door and into his Alfa Romeo, Bernadette was happy to collapse in the back seat.

As he navigated the dark country roads leading back to town, Niccolo asked, "Is it time yet, *cugino*?"

Bernadette let her eyes drift shut as Rocky filled Niccolo in on everything. His war history with Hamish. Seeing his old friend incognito at the bar. Hamish's work as a whistleblower. Seeing him with Passero and Fanucci that first night. How the Police Commissioner had stopped to talk to Hamish, and then how the others all left before Hamish did, meaning any one of them could have been waiting for him at the Loggia. One of them or a hundred others because it seemed Hamish had spoken to half the town in the days before he died.

Rocky told him how, from what little he'd learned before Hamish's death, Hamish had seemed particularly interested in the value of old violins, and how Gustaf Braun and Helmut Roth had told them about false authentication scams.

At that, Niccolo nodded wordlessly, eyes fixed on the road.

Rocky continued with how Gustaf Braun was not taken in by Fanucci's seemingly iron clad reputation for authentications. And now Fanucci had an interesting old violin on offer, a Guarneri that everyone involved was scrambling to own. Including some of the Cremona Crown contestants.

Rocky told him how they found the list of names in Hamish's room – skipping over the part about how they had broken into the room – then described how the people on the list all seemed to have something to do with Fanucci's violin authentications, and finally how, when they had tracked down Jeremy, they found he and Hamish had been planning to confront Fanucci this week at Mondo Musica for giving out false certificates of authenticity.

As Rocky's story unfolded, Niccolo sank lower in his seat. But at this last piece of news, he sat straight up. "You should have told me this last night!"

"I was planning on telling you. Soon," Rocky said. "But I wanted to get a bit more evidence."

"Well I think you got that tonight!" Nicco exclaimed.

"Yes. The car that chased us into the water... I've seen it around town. A green Lada station wagon. It was at Fanucci's party."

"I've seen it too," Niccolo said. "It really stands out."

"Do you know who it belongs to?" Rocky asked.

"No. But I'm going to find out."

There was a moment of silence, then Niccolo sighed. "Is there anything else I should know?"

Rocky hesitated, then said, "The problem is, there are other people with motive and opportunity, but the main suspects are Fanucci, Passero and Cassiglio. I think somehow they are in this together."

"That would make sense," Niccolo agreed. "The dealer, the craftsman and the moneyman."

Bernadette roused herself enough to add, "But even some of the Crown contestants are after the violin. They were there too the night Hamish was killed. Jay and Tatiana's handler, Mirela Florescu."

"Are you really considering them?" Niccolo asked, making eye contact with her in the dark car through the rear-view mirror.

She shrugged. "I don't think we can rule them out. We saw them both looking at the Guarneri in Fanucci's booth at Mondo Musica. Jay is ambitious and is determined to get that violin. And Mirela seems to have a personal attachment to it that I haven't quite figured out yet."

Niccolo sighed and rubbed his eyes with his fingers. "Is *that* all?"

"That's all," she said, and glanced at Rocky, who nodded in agreement. She didn't want to tell Niccolo about her feelings, how the spells and trances seemed to be brought on by the sound of the violin. Or how she sensed Mirela's connection to the violin. No, she wouldn't tell him, not if she could help it. Rocky was one thing, but Niccolo was something else altogether.

By now they were idling outside the Hotel Cremona. Rocky reached for the door handle.

"Be careful," Niccolo said seriously.

"I will," Rocky said as he climbed out of the car.

Niccolo put his hand on the back of Rocky's seat to prevent him from letting Bernadette out. "No. I mean it, *cugino*. These guys have already killed twice, and now they are after you. You are lucky you made it out of the water alive. Go back to interviewing your contestants and leave the murder investigation to the police."

Looking his cousin in the eye, Rocky waited a beat, then said, "You're right. They mean business. We'll be careful."

Nicco released the seat and Rocky helped Bernadette climb out. As they stood on the stairs of the hotel entrance,

Nicco rolled down the window and called out, "I mean it. Keep out of it."

Rocky raised a hand in salute to his cousin and ushered Bernadette in through the hotel door.

She started toward the elevator, then noticed Rocky hesitate inside the door.

"Coming up?" she asked.

"You go ahead. I just have a couple of things to see to."

She blew out a frustrated sigh. "You're going to see Passero, aren't you?"

"I need to find out what he wants to say."

Bernadette marched back across the lobby and opened the door. "It's getting late. We'd better get going."

Chapter 48

The rain had stopped and it was almost midnight when they headed out to Passero's shop, but with Mondo Musica in full swing, a festive atmosphere hung over the town. Even now, restaurants were open and the street-side tables were full. Piazza Roma, though, was dark and spooky, the path haunted by shifting shadows created by moonlight on the leaves overhead. Bernadette looked back over her shoulder more than once and was glad to leave the dark cover and cross the street to the row of shops.

Overhead lights dimly illuminated the street. With no restaurants on the block and all the stores closed, the side-walk was deserted. The window of Passero's shop was dark, as was the floor above, but looking up, Bernadette could see lights blazing in his private, second storey apart-ment. She thought she saw a light burning at the back of Fanucci's shop next door, but couldn't tell if anyone was there.

The unlit street entrance to the staircase to Passero's apartment was an uninviting black hole in the façade of the building. They hesitated in front of it, and Bernadette was relieved when Rocky said, "I still have Mia's key. Let's go in through the store."

"What do you think Passero wants?" Bernadette asked softly.

"I don't know," Rocky said as he unlocked the door. "Let him take the lead."

Bernadette followed him into the shadowy showroom. Streetlights shining in through the window threw enough illumination for them to find their way past the empty glass cases to the foot of the open staircase against the brick wall.

It was brighter at the top of the stairs where the street-lights shone directly in through the large semi-circular window casting gothic shadows onto the scene of work benches, hand tools and the skeletal ribs of a cello lean-ing against the wall. A chill crept up Bernadette's spine. She felt like they had stumbled into a seventeenth century workshop and half-expected a violinmaker's ghost to ma-terialize from the shadows.

The room was at least twenty feet high and above them, heavy footsteps could be heard crossing the floorboards that formed the ceiling. Her gaze met Rocky's. He'd heard it too. He took her hand and led her to the second set of stairs at the back of the workshop. These were narrower and ricketier than the first staircase and every step creaked as they slowly climbed. At the top, a small, dark landing faced a worn wooden door, the paint flaking off in patches.

"Maybe we should have gone in the other door," Bernadette said in a stage whisper.

"No, this is right. I've been here before."

Of course he had.

Rocky glanced back at her, then knocked.

Instantly the door swung open, as if Passero had been waiting for them. Bernadette sucked in a breath at the sight of the Maestro, silhouetted against the attic light. His grisly beard reached halfway down his chest and long white hair cascaded over his shoulders. Wearing a full-sleeved white shirt protected by a worn leather apron, he could have been a reincarnation of Guarneri himself.

Passero quickly ushered them inside. "*Sei tu. Si accomodi.* Come in." He stuck his head out to scan the staircase behind them to reassure himself that they were alone, then quickly closed the door. "Thank you for coming."

Bernadette took a quick look around. They stood in a large attic with sloped ceilings, the size of the entire building. Three strategically spaced lightbulbs hung from the rafters, leaving the edges and corners of the room deep in shadow. The space obviously served as both workshop and living accommodation: a workbench with tool racks was set up by the front window, a dusty old sofa stood in the center of the room and, in the back, she saw what looked like a sleeping area. Sawdust coated everything and tickled her nose.

They stood in an awkward circle in the middle of the room, the bare bulb above their heads casting stark shadows that turned their faces into carnival masks.

"Mia said you wanted to talk to us," Rocky began.

"*Sì*, yes. But we don't have much time." Passero glanced across the shop at another door in what Bernadette calculated must be the brick wall between his and Fanucci's buildings.

Passero rubbed his hands together. "Thank you for coming," he said again. He seemed eager to talk, but unsure of how to begin. Then his shoulders slumped and he shook his head. "Everything is gone very bad. This is not supposed to be. Not murder."

Bernadette's heart beat rapidly in her chest.

"Do you know who murdered Amos Ballantyne?" Rocky asked eagerly.

"Not murder," Passero repeated, shaking his head and wringing his hands. "I did help, all the years, but just working on the *violini*. Make them old. No one was supposed to die."

Rocky tried again. "Did you meet Amos Ballantyne?"

"He came by the shop asking about the old violins. Many people do, but he was *molto insistente.*"

"Very insistent," Rocky automatically translated for Bernadette.

"*Si*. Is dangerous, *colpire la bestia.*"

"To poke the beast."

"I tried to tell him, be careful, but he did not listen."

Three knocks on the door across the room startled them all. "Hide," Passero said quietly, but with underlying urgency in his voice as he looked frantically around the spacious room.

He grabbed Bernadette's arm and dragged her over to the bedroom area, with Rocky following close behind. Passero pushed them both toward the brick wall and whisked a floor-to-ceiling velvet curtain partway across the room.

The heavy drape provided a dark corner beside a dresser in the dim bedroom area. Rocky pressed Bernadette against the wall, then he pulled out his phone and turned on the recording app.

Passero crossed the room. "*Vengo, vengo.*"

Bernadette couldn't see past Rocky and the curtain, but heard the door open and a back-and-forth in Italian as the newcomer hustled into the room. She recognized the newcomer's voice – it was Fanucci.

The energy in the room shifted. He had brought the violin. She just knew it. There was something about that particular violin. Her body tingled every time she was in its presence. And it definitely had a presence. It was something she didn't sense with other instruments or, for that matter, most inanimate objects. Something she only sensed in the presence of ancient artifacts and religious icons.

Because that was the thing. This instrument was *animate*. It had a spirit. A soul. And now, if she listened carefully, she could hear a faint tinkle in the air of something that was not quite music, but was close.

Fanucci had the Guarneri.

Chapter 49

Using one finger, Rocky pulled the curtain aside an inch from where it touched the wall, creating a space that afforded him a narrow peek at the workshop area.

Fanucci walked into the room, talking non-stop about being late, meeting people. How it was important to get this business finished and over with, and then to lie low for a while.

He set a black violin case on the workbench and flicked open the latches, all the while continuing his barrage in Italian. "The student will never know the difference. Better him than the Romanian woman."

"Mirela," Passero said.

"Yes, stupid woman. She doesn't want to pay. Some story about how the violin belongs to her family."

"Roma," Passero said.

"I should have known she was a *zingara*." Fanucci spat the word.

A doorbell buzzed, and Passero crossed to an intercom on the wall by a third door at the back of the room that Rocky hadn't noticed before. He squeezed back against

Bernadette, pushing her farther into their hidden nook. Behind him, he heard her suck in a breath.

"*Entrare,*" Passero said into the intercom. He glanced over his shoulder in Rocky's direction but must have been satisfied they were out of sight because a moment later, he opened the door, and Jay and Gloria stepped inside. Jay was carrying another black violin case.

"*Buona sera,*" Passero said, stepping to the side and effectively blocking their view of Rocky and Bernadette's hiding spot. He quickly led the pair around the curtain and into the workshop.

Fanucci greeted them effusively in both Italian and English. "*Ciao, ciao!* My most esteemed contestant! Here to collect the noble *violino* with which you are sure to win the Cremona Crown."

A bit thick, but Jay seemed to eat it up.

"Perhaps, perhaps," he said, but had no time for modest protestations. The open case on the bench was pulling him like a magnet.

Fanucci turned on a spotlight above and the violin glowed as if lit by a celestial beam.

"May I?" Jay asked in a whispered breath.

"Of course. It is soon to be yours. If you have brought the money. And the violin to trade."

"Here's my violin," Jay said setting his case – which to Rocky's eye was identical to Fanucci's – on the bench. "And a bank draft for the balance." He reached into his back pocket, pulled out an envelope and lay it on top of his case.

Gloria watched the scene unfold, eyes shining as if her dreams were about to be realized. She seemed as bewitched

by the instrument as Jay was, as if it were the key to his
– no, their – future. A key that would unlock a life of
international travel and acclaim.

Fanucci spoke quickly, as if he wanted to get the trans-
action over and done and get the hell out. Passero stood
back, wringing his hands and glancing every so often at the
curtain.

A sudden movement by the open door caught Rocky's
eye and Mirela swept into the room, her magenta coat
swirling. She, too, carried a violin case, much like the ones
on the bench.

The group in the workshop turned in surprise.

"Ah, I see you have my violin," she said, walking boldly
up to the violin in the open case.

Fanucci frowned, Passero cringed, and Jay blustered,
"It's too late. I have already bought it." He reached out and
closed the lid of the case, snapping the locks securely.

Bernadette rubbed her nose with her finger; the tickle of
dust was getting stronger.

"Pah," Mirela said in disdain. "Many people have
bought and stolen that violin over the last century, but it
has never been theirs. It has always rightfully belonged to
my family."

"It is a Guarneri," Jay said scornfully. "I doubt your
family could ever afford an instrument like that."

Mirela laughed. "You are all fools. It is not a Guarneri; it
is a forgery."

Jay and Gloria both gasped.

Fanucci, although red-faced with anger at the intrusion,
did not look particularly surprised by her announcement.

"It is not a forgery. It is a Guarneri *del Gesù*. I have papers to prove it."

"You can keep your papers," Mirela said with a dismissive wave of her hand. "We all know what they are worth." She set her violin case on the bench with the others.

"That violin is a most beautiful forgery, made by my great-grandfather, the most famous Roma violin maker of last century. He copied all of the famous Italian makers of the golden age. After all, for centuries they came to Mures Valley, our home in Transylvania, to buy our wood. In the golden age, they called it, 'Little Cremona.' Through the centuries the art of Roma violin making continued there. My great-grandfather had much old wood to duplicate the famous violins. His violins were sought after by musicians around the globe.

"But this one is special. This one my family kept. My great-grandfather imbued it with Roma magic that I feel course through me when I play." Her voice had risen to a crescendo, then dropped to a hushed tone. "It was stolen by Ceauşescu's government in the nineteen seventies, but I am here to reclaim it, in the name of my family," she finished triumphantly.

"I don't thinks so," Fanucci said, drawing his portly body up to its full, unfortunate height. "I have already sold it to this young man. The deal has been struck."

Mirela's eyes narrowed, and she whipped a small but deadly pistol out of the folds of her remarkable coat. "*I* don't think so, you silly man. Hand it to me and I will be on my way."

At that moment, Jay and Fanucci both reached for the envelope on the bench, grabbing it in a tug of war between them. The dealer hardly knew which way to look as his plan fell to pieces before his eyes. The money was all that really mattered.

In the confusion, Mirela grabbed a case, spun towards the door, and suddenly jerked to a stop.

A sonorous voice echoed from the foyer beyond the door. "I will take the violin now."

Everyone in the workshop froze as Commissioner Grassi stepped into the room, a revolver in his hand.

That was the moment Bernadette couldn't hold it in any longer. She sneezed.

Grassi's eyes swept across the room to where Rocky and Bernadette were huddled in the dim corner.

He flicked his gun in their direction. "You two, come out."

Rocky put a hand on Bernadette's back, at the same time slipping the phone into the dresser drawer behind her. Then he followed her out into the room.

What, he wondered, was Grassi doing here? Would he straighten everything out and arrest Fanucci for something, forgery or possibly even murder, or was he in on the scheme? If only they'd had more time with Passero before Fanucci arrived, they might have learned who murdered Hamish. Rocky felt sure Passero had been ready to tell them everything he knew. And he seemed to know a lot.

Suddenly Jay wrenched the envelope containing the cheque out of Fanucci's hand, grabbed his violin case and took a step back, outside the circle, away from Fanucci. "I don't know what these men have done, Commissioner, but so far, no deal has been made. I will just take my own violin and ..." he inclined his head toward the open door through which they had entered.

Grassi must have believed him because he nodded brusquely. Jay and Gloria ran for the exit.

This Rocky could understand. Better to keep foreigners out of this mess. At this point all Jay and Gloria knew was that Grassi was the police.

Mirela stood still as a statue in the middle of the room.

"And you," Grassi said to her. "You can leave too."

She was out the door before the words were out of his mouth. Rocky heard Bernadette gasp beside him, but his focus remained laser sharp on Grassi.

Normal police procedure would have caused the Commissioner to keep Mirela there to interrogate her. But the jury was still out about which side Grassi was on.

As soon as Mirela disappeared through the door, Fanucci growled at Grassi in Italian. "You idiot! Put that gun away. Haven't you done enough damage?"

"You told me the next violin would be mine," Grassi spat back, also in Italian. "In fact, you told me the last *two* violins would be mine, but you sold them and pocketed the money. You and your partner. I have looked the other way long enough. This time it *is* mine."

Ha! Just as Rocky suspected. Grassi had been turning a blind eye to the forgery ring in the hope of getting one of the "famous" violins for himself.

Grassi raised the gun and aimed it directly at Fanucci's chest. "Hand it over. Now."

"What are you going to do," Fanucci asked. "Kill us all? You have already made enough of a mess killing Ballantyne and the British violinist."

"I did not kill Jeremy Reynolds. That was *your* friend, Cassiglio." Grassi snorted. "Or his goons."

Rocky had heard enough to unravel the story, but he didn't see how this meeting could end. Grassi seemed to have forgotten he and Bernadette were there. Rocky could feel her quivering beside him. Slowly, he moved to position himself between Grassi's gun and Bernadette. He tried to think back to his previous encounters with the Commissioner. Did Grassi know Rocky understood Italian? If not, the Commissioner might dismiss them too.

Grassi grabbed the remaining violin case off Passero's workbench. Then he swung the gun around and aimed it at Rocky. They stood ten feet apart at the most. It would be a sure shot.

"You two are a problem," he continued in Italian. "I am not fooled, Detective Falconi. Yes, I know who you are. I search every suspicious person who comes into my jurisdiction. An American detective *and* Ispettore Falconi's cousin? Of course you would search for the killer when your old *friend* Hamish Gladstone is murdered. Yes, I did a thorough search on you. And Signor "Ballantyne." And your partner. Although for her, it is bad luck to be your friend."

That answered the question of what Grassi knew.

"She doesn't know anything," Rocky said in Italian. His palms were sweating, but he tried to keep his voice calm. "She is no threat to you. She doesn't understand any Italian. Let her go."

"No, I'm afraid Senior Fanucci is going to have to kill you both. Just like he killed Mr. Ballantyne. Then I will have to expose his ring of thieves."

Grassi looked at Passero. "I am sorry Alessandro, old friend. I don't think I will be able to keep your name out of it. In a few minutes I will call my precinct for assistance."

"No need to call," a voice echoed into the room through the doorway to Passero's shop, and Niccolo stepped into the room, a gun in his hand, pointed at Grassi.

Grassi swung around and fired a round that ricocheted off the old wall sending shards of brick flying in all directions.

Immediately the door from staircase to the street burst open and two armed police officers leaped into the room, weapons drawn.

Faster than Rocky would have thought a man of his weight could move, Grassi grabbed Bernadette, pressing a beefy arm across her neck and his gun to her temple.

"*Sparerò!*" he said. *I'll shoot!*

Bernadette was pale as a ghost, her eyes, wide with fright, locked beseechingly on Rocky. His heart thudded painfully in his chest.

No one moved as the Police Commissioner dragged Bernadette towards the door to Fanucci's building. But foolishly, Grassi couldn't leave without one last look at *his* violin.

It was all the opening Rocky needed. With one leap he grabbed Grassi's gun arm and wrenched it away from Bernadette's head. The gun fired. The bullet pinged off the brick wall behind them.

Two TCP officers charged through the door from Fanucci's building, grabbing Grassi from behind and twisting the gun from his hand. Grassi looked frantically around the room, then realized there was no escape. It was over. He slumped in their grasp, releasing Bernadette who fell into Rocky's arms.

Quickly she righted herself and threw her arms around his neck, giving him a smacking kiss on the cheek. "My hero!"

"Anytime," he said, grinning at her adrenaline-fueled reaction, but happy to keep a protective arm around her waist just the same.

Chapter 50

I t was late when the police and the three arrested men left for the Questura, after first stationing a guard at the entrance to both premises.

Rocky and Bernadette were ready to call it a night, but Niccolo said he would be at the station until morning, writing his report.

"Your timing was perfect," Rocky told him. "How did you know we were here?"

Niccolo rolled his eyes theatrically. "Of course I knew you would come here. So I followed you. When everyone started arriving, I called for backup. I figured something was going down."

"I think Passero was going to tell us everything," Rocky said. "He started to talk, but then Fanucci arrived. He'd set up a meeting with Jay and Gloria. Mirela showing up was pretty much a wild card."

"I hope Passero won't be in too much trouble," Bernadette said. "I think he was just on the periphery of the ring. He obviously wasn't making much money from it. And he does such good work helping the young luthiers."

"Don't worry. We will figure it out. We've got some of the ring leaders now."

"But not Cassiglio," Rocky said.

Niccolo's eyes narrowed and his mouth pressed into a firm line. "No, once again, he has managed to not be in the room when the trouble breaks out. But I might be able to get enough from Fanucci to press charges. He is sweating like a pig, but perhaps is too afraid of the Mafia to talk. We might be able to get Cassiglio as an accessory to Jeremy Reynolds' murder, though. And we may have enough to charge him with money laundering or racketeering charges. That is not my jurisdiction. It is in the hands of the Financial Police. With your testimony, though, we can definitely charge Grassi with Hamish's murder."

"Did you suspect Grassi?"

"I wouldn't have thought he'd commit murder, but I knew he was turning a blind eye to the racket Cassiglio and, I suspected, Fanucci had going. This will put him away for a long time."

"So the Commissioner's job is open," Rocky said with a tilt of his head and a raised eyebrow.

Niccolo smiled, but didn't comment.

"Why did Grassi let Mirela go?" Bernadette asked.

"She is Roma. He knew she would never talk to the police. She wouldn't report anything she saw or heard. And the fewer witnesses the better for what he had in mind."

"Do you think the violin really did belong to her family?" Bernadette asked.

"Hard to say what is the truth," Niccolo said. "If it does, she can register for repatriation with the government of Romania."

Bernadette's heart sank. She felt strongly that Mirela had been telling the truth, that her great-grandfather had built the violin. She'd felt the magic Mirela spoke of whenever the violin was in the room. Of course, Fanucci had known right away that it was not a Guarneri, but it was such a good forgery that, with papers from him, it would pass as an old master's violin.

"I wonder why Grassi wanted the violin so badly?" Rocky mused.

"He wanted to belong," Niccolo explained. "He grew up here as the son of a police officer, going to school with sons of the violin community. With them, but never one of them. Finally, this was his chance, and Hamish Ballantyne would ruin everything. Bring the whole lot of them down. Grassi included." He shrugged. "You'd have to grow up here to understand."

Or maybe, Bernadette thought, he just felt the magic.

Sunday Afternoon, Day Six

Chapter 51

The next afternoon, the final concert of the Cremona Crown Competition played out at *Teatro Ponchielle*, the two-hundred-and-fifty-year-old grand opera hall. Bernadette snuggled into the plush, red velvet seat and gazed up at the five tiers of gilt-edged balconies that ringed the orchestra seating. On the stage, the orchestra was warming up, discordant notes echoing into the glorious space.

The contest was down to four finalists: Cordelia, the British competitor, Angelo, the Italian, and Jay and Tatiana.

Jay had looked morose that morning at breakfast. Bernadette felt sure he'd thought his dreams of fame and fortune flew out the window when Commissioner Grassi walked through the door into Passero's loft. Unfortunately, Jay was not mature enough to rise above the setback, and his lackluster final performance showed the strain. The other two contestants played well, as expected, but Tatiana, the final contestant to perform, was the one Bernadette was waiting to hear.

In the interval before Tatiana took center stage, Niccolo slipped into the empty seat beside Bernadette.

"There was a mix up with the violins last night," he said quietly, staring straight ahead at the stage.

Bernadette's heart sank to her stomach. She'd known at the time – Mirela had left with the wrong violin. Or the right violin. Bernadette had felt the quality of its presence, the tingle in the room, disappear when Mirela swept out the door.

She had to admit, she was rooting for Mirela to wind up with it in the end. Bernadette had believed her when she said it belonged to her family, and even though official repatriation was a better way to go, it was a slow and often expensive process. Mirela did not strike her as someone willing to jump through that many bureaucratic hoops.

Her thoughts were interrupted when Tatiana stepped onto the stage. Bernadette felt a tingle go through her. Anticipation, or something more? The girl lifted the violin to her shoulder, clamped it in place with her chin, raised the bow and began to play.

With the first strong notes of Brahms Violin Concerto, a delicious chill swept over Bernadette. Tatiana had the violin.

Bernadette glanced at Niccolo, but he had crossed his arms on his chest and closed his eyes. She didn't know what he had planned, but it seemed he was going to let this play out. At least until the concert was over.

So Bernadette closed her eyes and let the music, wild and free, sweep her away. Tatiana's fingers flew up and down the neck of the violin, each note ringing out crisp and clear. Under Tatiana's bow Bernadette could feel the underlying flavor of the Hungarian folk melodies the concerto was based on. In the slow, mournful sections, she managed to draw every exquisite emotion out of the violin before building back up to a rousing finish.

The audience exploded with applause bringing Bernadette out of her trance. Up on the stage, Tatiana, eyes closed, let out a breath of satisfaction, then opened her eyes and her face lit up with a smile. Bernadette realized she had never seen the girl smile before, but now she was beaming. Tatiana looked quizzically at the violin in her hand and seemed to give it a little shake of recognition. Probably not enough for most people to see, but enough for Bernadette.

Tuesday evening, Day Eight

Chapter 52

Two nights later, Bernadette met Rocky in the hotel bar for their last evening meal together.

"Quite a week," he said, holding up his drink to clink with her glass of sparkling Prosecco. "I thought it would be easy, fun." *Maybe even romantic.* "Not another murder to solve."

Bernadette grinned. "It was fun." She shrugged. "Most of it, anyway."

She set her glass down on the shiny oak bar. "Did they ever catch Mirela?" Rocky had met Niccolo for a final coffee that afternoon while she'd been catching up on her notes.

He shook his head. "She got away. Must have had a car or accomplices with a car. Not surprising considering the Roma network in Italy."

"I'm kind of glad," Bernadette admitted. "I believed her story about her great-grandfather."

"Ya," Rocky said skeptically. "It was quite a story."

Bernadette sighed. "Well, *I* think it was a happy ending. I'm glad Tatiana won. I thought she was the best, and she'd told me her mother is seriously ill and they needed the prize money for meds. Apparently they are not easy to come by in Romania, even now."

Rocky nodded. "She seemed like a good kid. I doubt she knew anything about the violin."

"But nice of Mirela to let her play it for the concert. That was quite a risk."

"Mirela had it all figured out. She switched violins after the performance and made a clean getaway while Tatiana was receiving her prize."

They were silent for a few moments, then Bernadette took a sip of her drink and said, "And you found Hamish's killer."

"No, *we* did," he corrected with a crooked smile. "Partner."

Bernadette grinned. She still felt a thrill when he called her that.

"I have enough material for more than one article," she said. "We'll have to talk over our ideas after we get home."

"Tomorrow," he said.

She nodded in reply, but something tingled in the atmosphere around them.

"Do you have to go home right away?" he asked. "The Italian riviera is still nice at this time of year."

She moaned softly, and bit her lip. She wanted to stay but...

"I do. I have to go. It would be nice," she admitted, sinking into the dark depths of his gaze for a moment. But only a moment, then she looked away. "My son has been calling, and my mom has to leave for a conference in Seattle the day after I get back, so I'm on mom-duty again."

Rocky nodded, downed his drink. "Next time then." He looked across the room, then stood up, holding out his hand for hers. "I think our table is ready."

Next time, she thought. *You bet.*

The End

Stay up to date with Rocky and Bernadette's adventures by joining my readers group. You can find background and photos of the actual scenes on my website – https://www.JM.HudsonMystery.com

Dear Readers,

Thank you for following Bernadette and Rocky on assignment in Italy.

First of all, just so we're clear, ALL OF THE CHAR-ACTERS IN THE BOOK ARE TOTAL FABRICA-TIONS AND NOT BASED ON ANYONE I MET IN CREMONA.

ALSO, NO PORTION OF THIS BOOK WAS WRITTEN USING AI TECHNOLOGY.

I have a family connection to the violin business and have been to Cremona a number of times, so it was a natural place for our heroes to visit in their second book, especially since Rocky has family there.

Cremona is a fascinating, beautiful, historic city in northern Italy, just south of Milan, with all of the medieval and Renaissance history and architecture I mention in the book as well as the Roman and pre-Roman history as well.

It is the home of Stradivari, Amati, and all of the violin makers I mention in the story. I have tried to be honest with my portrayal of this violin world, but any mistakes are mine and mine alone.

The Cremona Crown Competition is a total fiction, but Mondo Musica is an annual trade show that is just as chaotic (to my ears) as portrayed! I went a few times to help a friend with his booth and would love to go back.

I tried to capture the convoluted police structure in Italy as best I could. Art is everywhere, in churches, public and private spaces, and art and artifact theft is rampant.

The Mures Valley is a real place in Transylvania and in the 17th and 18th centuries was known as 'Little Cremona' because many violin makers of the Golden Age there went to source instrument wood. It still has a thriving musical instrument trade and is home to a great concentration of Roma people.

Rocky and Bernadette's next assignment will be in northern Scotland. For background to the series, pictures of Cremona and news of when the next book will be released, sign up for my readers group on my website at https://www.JudithHudsonAuthor.com

Thank you for reading Rocky and Bernadette mysteries.
Judith Hudson

Thank you!

W riting a book takes a village, and I am indebted to the people who took the time to read the manuscript in its various forms and gave me their honest feedback.

To Janet and John Whittam who read the manuscript before it was even finished. I will send them a copy so they can see who-done-it in the end.

To Joanne Morris and Eve Devi, loyal readers who pointed out a few problems while I still had time to solve them.

To Ann Elliott-Goldschmid, previously first violinist with the famous Lafayette String Quartet for its full 38 years and Associate Professor at University of Victoria, who gave me necessary practical advice and insight into what happens at violin competitions, for which she has many times been an adjudicator.

John Caldwell and Natasha Pow for their thoughtful reading of the final draft.

And my ARC readers for their comments and reviews!

And I have to thank Stephanie Webb, my trusted editor who was with me through the whole process, from story idea to the final draft, reminding me what I meant to say, often before I said it. Thank you my friend.

But even with all of this help and advice, any errors in the book are entirely my own.

And of course, I have to thank you, my readers. I hope you enjoyed Rocky and Bernadette's second adventure. Stay tuned for their next adventure – Destination: Scotland!

Judith Hudson